BLURRED LINES

BY DEEZIGN MYSTERIES BOOK 2

DEE MCQUEEN

Dear Kenzie,
I hope you enjoy
Reading the Book as
much as I enjoyed writing
it :)

Dee McQueen

4/20/24

BY DEEZIGN MYSTERIES

Blurred Lines - By Deezign Mysteries Book 2
Copyright @ 2023 Dee McQueen
Cover Design By Rose Miller
Editor Tameka Brown

For more information, email Deemcqueen@bydeezignmysteries.com

BLURRED LINES

BY DEEZIGN MYSTERIES BOOK 2

1

KAREN LASALLE PROM DAY

2003...

Today was supposed to be the pinnacle of my year — the senior prom— and I was going with my high school sweetheart, Sean McKnight. Who would have known that one phone call would lead to my murder?

"Good morning, Karen, It's Jordan. I really need to talk to you. I'm worried about Sean. Can you meet me at Gallup Park in about an hour?"

"Jordan, why can't you just tell me now?"

"Please Karen, Sean could be in a lot of trouble."

"Okay, I'll be there."

Why did I agree to go meet him? Jordan Kimmble is Sean's best friend and has been since kindergarten.

I put on my Apple Bottom jeans, ran downstairs, and gave my mom a kiss on her cheek. I told her I was running out really quick and would be right back.

When I pulled up, Jordan was waiting for me. He waved me over to his car.

"Ok Jordan, why is Sean in trouble?"

Without saying a word, Jordan pulled me close to him and

started to kiss me. I tried to push him away, but he was too strong. It seemed like it lasted forever. I heard someone coming, and I wanted to scream, but I couldn't.

"Jordan! Karen! What are you two doing? yelled Chanda Powers.

Crying, I said, "Chanda, Jordan just..."

"I saw everything, Karen! You pulled Jordan towards you and started kissing him!"

"No, No, that's not what happened!"

"How could you two do this to Sean? And what about Courtney? This is going to break her heart!"

Courtney Collins was Chanda's best friend. She started dating Jordan when he became the varsity basketball team captain, and they were supposed to be going to prom together.

Jordan pleaded with Chanda, "Please don't say anything. You saw what happened...it was Karen! She was flirting with me, and it just happened. I promise I will tell Courtney everything after prom. You know how long she has been looking forward to going."

"You both have until after prom to tell Sean and Courtney, or I will!" Chanda sneered.

I turned around and ran to my car. The radio started playing, "So Gone," by Monica. I turned it off and just cried. I didn't pull off because my hands and knees were still shaking badly. I could not believe what just happened. *What if no one believes me? It's my word against Chanda and Jordan's.*

———

I went home and took a nap, then was awakened by a phone call from Sean. He told me that something happened between Jordan and Courtney, and now they weren't going to prom together; so Sean wanted Jordan to ride with us.

"No!! I do not want him riding with us, Sean."

"He's my best friend; I feel bad for him."

"He can't ride with us, and that's it."

I so badly wanted to tell Sean what happened. I know that he is going to be upset with me, but there is no way I am going anywhere near Jordan ever again.

My mom yelled up the stairs and told me my best friend, Montel Kingsley, was outside. I wiped the tears from my eyes and ran downstairs. I don't know why he is here. After our phone conversation last night, I didn't think he would ever talk to me again. Maybe Chanda told him about what happened at the park.

"Hi Montel."

Montel pointed his finger in my face and started to yell at me. He grabbed my arm and out of nowhere, my neighbor from across the street, Ms. Mary, yelled at him, and he ran away.

Ms. Mary walked over to me and said, "Child, are you ok? Did he hurt you?"

"No ma'am, I'm fine. He is just upset, that's all. Thank you!"

I went back into the house. My mother asked what was wrong, and I told her that it was nothing. I closed my bedroom door and lay across my purple and pink butterfly comforter. I felt a buzz in my pocket and pulled out my pink Motorola flip phone. It was Sean calling me.

"Hi, Karen, I just wanted you to know that I did what you asked. I told Jordan that he can't ride with us to prom. I hope that makes you happy. I'll be there to pick you up at 6:30pm."

I said, "Thank you, Sean, I'll see you then."

———

We walked into prom; our colors were green and gold. It took us a while to find Sean a bow tie that matched my dress, but we finally did. We started to dance to, "Hey Ya," by Outkast. Sean was a much better dancer than I. I was having so much fun, that I almost forgot about what happened earlier that day between Jordan and I...until I saw him talking to Chanda and Montel at the dessert table.

Chanda saw me looking at them, and she gave me an evil stare. I hate her. We walked off the dance floor, I started to talk to a class-mate and Sean headed towards the dessert table, because he wanted to talk to Jordan. As he walked up, he heard Montel and Jordan arguing and ran over to them right when Jordan threw a punch. I headed towards the commotion, and Chanda yelled at me, telling me that it was all my fault — she said that they were fighting about me. Chanda showed me a picture, and immediately my heart began to race. It was a picture of Jordan kissing me...she said that after tonight everyone would know the kind of girl I was.

I tried to rip it out of her hand, but she was too fast and pulled it away, sticking it into her handbag. I went from sad to angry...*who does she think she is?* Tears began to roll down my cheek.

Sean turned around and asked me why I was crying, and I told him everything was my fault. I felt like I was going to throw up. I had to get out of there, so I ran outside to get some fresh air. I headed in the direction of the parking lot. I could not remember where Sean parked, but I just needed to get away...and that's where I ran into my murderer.

2

Sean McKnight had been anticipating this class reunion for the last few months. He did not RSVP or inform anyone that he was attending it. He wanted to catch everyone off guard. He was so close to finally solving the murder of his high school sweetheart.

Sean could vividly see Karen lying in the puddle of blood and the rips in her dress from the knife that was plunged into her chest 4 times...he could hear the screams and crying from the large crowd that ran outside from prom, and the feeling of bricks on his chest as he gasped for air while holding her lifeless body.

Even though Sean was cleared of being a suspect, the shame and hurt still stung when he thought about it. His close friends and many in the community believed the lie that he killed Karen Lasalle, and that was something that Sean could not forgive. The most painful part was his grandmother; Sean loved her so much. She was all he had after his mother died. She reassured Sean that she did not believe the stories, but he could see the shame in her eyes. It was his grandmother who persuaded him to leave Michigan and go to stay with his aunt in Ohio after graduation. There is where he met his wife, Shelia, and where he went through the police academy.

Soon after graduating from the academy, Sean was offered a job in Rhode Island by an instructor at the academy, who was starting her new career as a captain.

Sean loved being a police officer, and he was good. He would occasionally call back to Michigan to find out if there were any new leads on the case, and the answer was always no. This was so upsetting to Sean because he knew that if Detective Montgomery had spent more time looking for the real murderer and less on trying to pin it on him because of a family feud, they may have found the person responsible. Even though everyone else had given up, Sean did not. His main goal was justice for Karen, but he wanted to, once and for all, clear his name and stop all the whispers. There were many people in his hometown who still believed that he killed Karen.

Now it has been 10 years since they graduated from high school, and the class reunion was quickly approaching. This would be the first time Sean went back to Ypsilanti since his grandmother's death.

———

"Good morning, Beautiful," Sean said, as he sat up giving Shelia a kiss on the lips.

Shelia stretched her arms over her head and replied, "Good morning, Sean, I can't believe Christopher slept all night long. With those teeth coming in, he has been clingy and waking up every night for the past few days."

With a smile, Sean said, "Shelia, that's because daddy's home. I can't believe our baby is two years old...time sure is flying. I hate to leave today for this reunion, but you know I have to."

Shelia exclaimed, "I know, I can't wait until this is all over. I don't want to share her with you anymore, Sean. You have been obsessed with finding Karen's murderer ever since I met you. I thought maybe when we started our family it would be different; I was wrong. Sean, promise me that after this, you will let her Rest in Peace. I want to be the only woman in your life. I'm done competing against her."

Sean swung his legs off the bed, into his black slippers and said, "How can you say that? You are my one and only love. There is no competition. I only want to bring Karen's murderer to justice, and I am sorry that you feel this way."

Without saying another word, he walked over to the closet, pulled his suitcase down and started to pack. He was irritated with Shelia; she knew how painful the subject was for him.

Shelia walked over to Sean, put her arms around him, laid her head on his back and said, "Sean I'm sorry. I know that this is something that you need to do. I do hope that this weekend gives you all the answers that you need, so that you can finally put this all in the past where it belongs."

Shelia ran into the bathroom and Sean ran behind her. She kneeled over the toilet and began throwing up. Sean grabbed a towel off the shelf, ran cold water over it and laid it across her neck. Shelia grabbed the rag and wiped her mouth. She looked flushed and her eyes were watery.

Smiling Shelia said, "I was going to wait to tell you when you got back home from the reunion, but I'm pregnant, Sean!!"

Sean pumped his fist and yelled, "YES, I would kiss you, but I need you to brush your teeth first." They both laughed, Sean smiled and pointed towards the toothbrush and nodded. Shelia slapped his shoulder and walked towards the sink.

The baby started crying, and Sean went to check on him so that Shelia could get herself together.

Sean always wanted a big family. He was an only child and didn't have a relationship with his father. He was always envious of Shelia and her family. She had 2 bothers and 2 sisters; both parents were still around, and she had tons of cousins.

Sean walked into Christopher's room. It looked bright because of the glowing stars that were placed on his ceiling in the shape of the

Big Dipper. He bent down and pulled Christopher toward him. Cradling his tiny head in his hand, Sean whispered, "Guess what, Son? You are going to be a big brother. I know that you are going to be the best big brother ever."

He rocked Christopher back to sleep and headed back to the bedroom to get dressed.

Sean had to report to the police station. He had recently been promoted to a detective and had new partner. The detective that trained him decided to retire because he wasn't happy with all the new changes the department was implementing.

Sean did not like change either, so he wasn't in a hurry to be introduced to his new partner. He heard about him, though. He was a street-smart detective that was being transferred over from narcotics and was a few years older than Sean.

Rumor had it, he was being transferred because he was dating his boss's daughter, and the relationship went sour. He started catching all the rookie's duties and assignments. He went to the union, and they were instrumental in getting him transferred.

I hope he doesn't think about dating our Captain's daughter. He would lose more than his job, Sean thought.

He ran downstairs with his tie halfway on, grabbed a bagel and coffee and ran out the door. Then, Sean turned around, ran back in, and gave Shelia and Christopher a kiss and bolted towards the door.

———

"Hey Paddington."

"How are you doing McKnight? You better high tail it to the Caps office. She and the new detective have been waiting for you."

Sean knew that the captain's pet peeve was when a person was not on time, and to her, being on time meant being 15 minutes early. In fact, she was known to embarrass officers who were late.

Sean knocked on the door and walked in.

The captain shouted, "McKnight you're late! I want you to meet Phillips."

Sean said, "Cap, I'm so sorry for being late."

He extended his hand towards Phillips and said," it is nice to meet you, Phillips. Looking forward to working with you when I get back."

Shaking Sean's hand, he replied, "Likewise., The captain speaks very highly of you."

"Now that we have the introductions out of the way, Phillips can you give me and McKnight a few minutes?"

Phillips nodded and walked out the door. McKnight was sure he was about to get chewed out by the captain.

Before she could say anything, he said, "Guess what, Cap? Shelia is pregnant! I know you hate it when someone is late, but she was puking. I had to help her, and then Christopher started to cry…"

She walked from behind her desk, gave Sean a big hug and said, "I'm so happy for you and Shelia, but you just used your one and only get-out-of-jail-free card. Don't be late again." She smiled and sat back down behind her desk.

Sean turned to walk away, and Cap said, "Sean, I hope you are able to find the answers you are looking for this weekend. Ever since I met you at the academy, this has been eating at you. If you need any assistance while you are there, please reach out and be safe. If your theory is correct that one of your former classmates at the reunion is a cold-blooded murderer, this could be very dangerous. Watch your six!"

The thought of one of Sean's old friends being a murderer made him sick to his stomach. He went to his desk, grabbed a few files, and then left to go home and grab his suitcase.

3

Sean opened the door and Shelia put her finger up to her mouth and looked down. On the floor lay two-year-old Christopher, fast asleep, and by the look of Shelia's expression, she was ready to lay on the floor next to him.

Sean wondered if Shelia was pregnant with a girl or another boy. He didn't care, though, he only wanted a healthy, happy baby, but Shelia wanted a girl. That's all she talked about after Christopher was able to walk and started getting into everything.

Sean grabbed his suitcase, walked over to Shelia and gave her a kiss. Shelia pulled away from Sean.

"What was that about, Shelia?"

"It doesn't matter, Sean. Bye, you have a plane to catch."

"My ride is not here yet. Talk to me..."

"I just thought after I told you I was pregnant you would change your mind and stay. You know how difficult my last pregnancy was, Sean."

Shelia had preeclampsia with Christopher, and for the last month of her pregnancy she was on bedrest. After she delivered Christopher, she had pregnancy-induced, congestive heart failure and her mom had to stay with them for two months to help take care of the baby.

Exhaling, Sean said, "Shelia, where is this coming from? When we talked this morning, you were fine with me leaving, and now you come to me with this. I will only be gone for three days."

Aggravated, Shelia said, "Sean, you are not hearing me. I know this is important to you. I just thought maybe when you found out that I was pregnant and had some time to think about it, you would change your mind about going. Don't worry about me and Christopher, we will be fine."

Grabbing Shelia's hands, Sean said, "Shelia, I love you, but I need to do this. It may be my only opportunity to finally find out who killed Karen. I don't know when I will be able to have all of my former classmates together again. I hope you can understand that."

Sean felt guilty leaving Shelia with Christopher for the weekend now that he knew she was pregnant, but he could not back out of going back home.

"If anything comes up and you can't get in touch with me, call the captain. I also let Ms. Parker know that I'll be out of town. She said that if you need any help with Christopher that she will come over or you can bring Christopher to her."

Rolling her eyes she said, "Ms. Parker wants to come 'help' so she can be nosey and tell all the neighbors how much I needed her and tell them everything that I do wrong as a mother."

Sean bent down, kissed Christopher on his forehead and said, "Daddy loves you. Take care of mommy while I'm gone."

There was a beep outside. It was Tony...he was an officer at the police department, there to give Sean a ride to the airport. Sean and Tony were in the academy together in Ohio. He and his wife had recently divorced. She was also a police officer, in the same station as Tony. It hurt too badly for Tony to see her every day. Especially since it was rumored that she had started dating a sergeant at their station. Sean talked Tony into moving to Rhode Island and working at the precinct with him.

Sean stopped at the door and said, "I love you, Shelia. I will call you when I land."

Sean got into Tony's 1975, cherry red Thunderbird. Tony and his dad worked on that car every summer for 4 years, and his dad gave it to him when he graduated from the police academy.

Tony yelled, "Hey!!! Be easy with my baby...don't slam the door, she doesn't like that!"

Sean rolled his eyes and tossed his suitcase in the back seat. The seats were shiny, like Tony had spent all morning cleaning the leather.

Tony was concerned about Sean. He could see the worry in his eyes. When they were in the academy, Sean told Tony about his girlfriend being murdered, and how he was a suspect but was cleared. Tony never asked any questions; he just allowed Sean to talk about it when he needed to.

Tony said, "You know you can share anything with me, man. I've shared everything with you, and you helped me out when I needed it most. Maybe it would help if you talked about it."

Sean took a deep breath, rubbed his brow, and said, "Tony man... that was the most horrible time of my life. Just thinking about it makes me sick."

"I get that, but maybe it will help you put some more of the pieces together by talking it out. You know you are going to need proof, not just your accusations, to solve the murder and remove any lasting doubts from everyone's mind that it was you."

Sean took a deep breath and said, "Maybe you're right."

4

SEAN MCKNIGHT PROM DAY
2003...

I just don't understand why Karen is making such a big deal about Jordan riding to prom with us. The three of us always do things together, so what's the problem today? I feel like I am betraying Jordan.

Jordan's girlfriend, Courtney Collins, was grounded, and her parents were not allowing her to go to prom. Jordan was upset about having to go alone, and I just didn't want my buddy to have to go by himself, so I invited him to ride with us. Maybe I should have asked Karen if she would mind, but it was just a 15-minute ride to the high school. I didn't think it would be a problem.

I probably could have handled it better when she told me she didn't want him to come, but now she wouldn't answer the phone. I'm going to try to call her again. Nope...straight to voicemail.

"Hey, Karen, this is Sean again...I'm leaving you another message. Please pick up the phone. This is not how I envisioned today going. The last thing that I want to do is fight with you right now. I know that I upset you, and if you don't want Jordan to ride with us, I'm okay with that. I will call him now and let him know. Please call me back."

I walked over to the oval mirror that my grandmother had mounted on the wall. It had been passed down from generation to generation and engraved on the back is our family tree. My name was the last to be added. I don't have any siblings; my mother was an only child, and since she died when I was fifteen, it would be up to me to have children and add their names to the empty leaves on the tree.

I'm looking in the mirror, practicing different ways I can tell Jordan that he has to find another way to prom. I might as well forget it. There is nothing I can say that will make my message less harsh. I could lie, but what could possibly be a good enough excuse?

My hands are so sweaty...this is the third time I've had to wipe them on my pants. I need to relax; maybe he will understand. I picked up my phone and slowly began to tap each number. The phone rang, and just when I thought about hanging up, Jordan answered.

"What's up, Sean! Are you ready for tonight? It is going to be epic! I know you are probably calling back to check on me, but I promise you I am going to have fun tonight even though Courtney is not coming."

Interrupting, I said, "Jordan, that's not why I'm calling. There is no easy way to say this."

"Alright then, spit it out, man! I don't have all day."

"You can't ride to prom with me and Karen tonight."

I removed the phone from my ear. I was expecting Jordan to start yelling at me any second, but he was silent.

"Look, it's not my idea. Karen is adamant about you not riding with us, and..."

"Just stop, Sean, you called me and offered me a ride, and now you tell me that I won't be able to ride with you. That's not right, man, don't worry about me...I'll figure it out."

Before I could get another word in, Jordan hung up on me. That did not go well at all. If the night keeps going this way, I won't have a girlfriend or a best friend.

I was walking back to my bed. I had a splitting headache and needed to lie down for a bit. Just as my head hit the pillow, my phone rang. I was hoping it was Jordan calling back to tell me that he understood, and we were still cool, but it was Karen. I sat the phone next to me and debated on whether or not to answer. If it was earlier, I would have picked it up right away. I'm not feeling her right now after my conversation with Jordan. I let it ring until it went to voicemail. I don't want to talk to her. I cannot believe that she is acting like this. Because of her, I broke a promise to my best friend. To make it even worse, she won't give me an explanation as to why she doesn't want Jordan to ride with us.

Even though I'm upset with her, I quickly gave in, picked up the phone and listened to her message:

"Sean, thank you! I know that you don't understand why I don't want Jordan to ride with us, but I promise I will explain everything after prom. I just...I just need you to understand that it is very important to me, and I have a very good reason. I know what your friendship with Jordan means to you, but I just don't know if he values it as much as you do. I hope you are not mad at me. I will call you after my hair appointment. I'm heading out to Salon Kimistry to get my hair done and then to Glowing with Ki for my makeup. I will be ready by 6:30. See you then."

After hearing Karen's voice, I relaxed. She said she would tell me everything after prom, and that is good enough for me. I decided to call her after I went to get my haircut. I like my hair the length it is – my sides are faded and curly on the top, but Karen wants me to cut in low for our pictures. I don't mind...I would do anything for Karen.

———

I decided to get someone else's perspective on the situation to make sure I wasn't tripping, so I asked the fellas at the barber shop how they would have handled it. Half of them agreed with me for going along with Karen. The other half said I was dead wrong for doing my best friend like that. One thing they all agreed on, is that if I wanted to enjoy prom, not to bring my issue up with Karen until after it was over.

I pulled into the driveway, and my grandmother was standing on the porch in her light blue, floral nightgown. She has been wearing that since I was a little boy. She said that my grandfather bought it for her, and when she wears it, she feels close to him. I could tell by the look on her face that something was wrong. She was waving her hand back and forth...I knew that meant that I needed to move quickly.

She said, "Courtney is in the kitchen waiting on you. That poor girl has been crying for the last ten minutes. I gave her some tea and homemade tea cakes hoping that would help calm her down."

My grandmother believed that there was no problem that tea and cookies could not solve.

I went into the kitchen, and Courtney sat there with red, puffy eyes. Her hair was in a high ponytail, and there was a wad of wet tissues sitting on the table in front of her. I hate to see any woman cry. It could be because of all the tears I watched my mother shed at the hands of her many abusive boyfriends, or it could be from the tears I saw my grandmother cry over my mother. Either way it was more than I could bear.

Courtney jumped up, ran over to me, and threw her arms around me. I began hugging her and patting her back to soothe her, but the longer I hugged her, the harder she sobbed.

I stepped back, put my hands on her shoulders and said, "Court, what's wrong?"

Wiping the tears away with her shirt sleeve, Courtney replied, "I hate Karen! She ruined my life. Did she tell you that she is the reason I can't go to prom? Can you believe Jordan is still going without me?"

"Courtney, Karen did not make you hit Jordan's car with a bat... you did that. I don't know why you are always so mean to her."

I watched as Courtney's sad countenance suddenly turned to rage; she began to yell at me. I tried to talk to her calmly, but the more I talked, the angrier she became. My grandmother, who had been standing by in the living room, came into the kitchen.

"What is all this hollering in my house about?" She said with both hands on her hips.

"I'm sorry, Mrs. McKnight." Courtney replied, and she ran out of the kitchen towards the front door.

My grandmother began to pat her foot with her hands still on her hips. My stomach was doing somersaults; I seemed to upset everyone today. Karen, Jordan, Courtney, and now my grandmother.

She said, "I'm not sure what that was all about, but I hope you are not the cause of that young lady's pain. I raised you better than that. Whatever it is, fix it!!" She turned away to walk up the stairs.

I wish I could fix it. I have no idea what is going on. All I know is I have been looking forward to prom for months, and now I just want today to be over with.

———————

Karen and I walked into prom; she looked beautiful in her long, green, form-fitting mermaid dress, gold shoes and accessories, and a beautiful corsage. I had on a cream suit, with a green bow tie and pocket square to match her dress. We were happy with how we looked. It took a while to find the right shades of green that matched. I told her we should just go with another color, but she wanted green, and once Karen sets her mind on something, there is no changing it.

While Karen and I danced, I tried not to think about the visit from Courtney and how upset she was, all the while blaming Karen for everything. *What is Karen hiding? Was the reason she didn't want Jordan to ride with us was that she feared him telling me something she doesn't want me to know?*

The more I thought about it, the more agitated I was getting. If Karen won't tell me, then I'm going to go straight to Jordan and ask him what was going on. The only problem is, I don't know if he will even talk to me after what I had done.

I scanned the room looking for Jordan. I began to walk towards the dessert table where Jordan, Chanda, and Montel were standing. It looked like he was arguing with Montel because they were nose to nose. I started to run over towards them. I want to let Jordan punch Montel; he is definitely the biggest jerk I ever met, but I don't want Jordan to get into any more trouble. He has been in two fights at school already this year...another suspension could cause him to lose his basketball scholarship.

Montel doesn't have to worry about anything like that. His family is very wealthy. His grandfather, Mathis Kingsley, is the CEO of Kingsley Corp and Montel's father, Craig, will soon be elected by the board to be CEO, so that Mathis could finally retire to Florida.

I was too late...Montel had pushed Jordan to the ground. Jordan jumped up and ran towards Montel, extended his arm and punched him in the nose. I made it over there just in time to catch Montel as he was falling backwards. He was struggling to get out of my arms to go back after Jordan. The hall monitor, Paul Stewart, ran over and grabbed Jordan.

Montel jerked away from me and went one way, while Paul took Jordan into the hallway.

Karen covered her face with her hands and began to cry.

"What's wrong, Karen?"

"Sean, you don't understand...this is all my fault. I never should have said anything to Montel. They got into that argument because of me."

"What do you mean, Karen? What is going on? You have been acting very weird all day, and then I get a surprise visit from Courtney, who was very upset, saying she couldn't come to prom because of you, and now this. What have you gotten yourself into?"

Karen ran out of the auditorium, and I ran behind her. Paul grabbed me as I was running past him. He asked if I saw what started the altercation between Montel and Jordan. I told him that I saw as much as he did. I answered a few more questions and turned to look for Karen.

I went towards the restrooms, and I ran into Chanda Powers. She told me that she saw Karen run outside. I ran out the back door; it was darker than usual...one of the lights in the back of the school was out. I started calling out for Karen, but she didn't answer. I think I see something on the ground, so I started running as fast I could towards it. I felt like my heart stopped beating. It was Karen, and she was lying in a pool of blood. My knees became weak, and I fell to the ground, I gently pulled her close to me and held her in my arms.

"HELP! HELP! SOMEONE, PLEASE HELP!" I screamed.

The auditorium door opened, and everyone started running over towards us.

5

Silence filled the car. Then Tony said, "Sean, I'm so sorry, that's horrible. You've been carrying a lot for a long time. I hope you get the closure you need this weekend."

Sean whispered, "Thanks for the ride. I'll get out here."

As Sean was walking into the airport, his phone rang. He looked down, and it was the call he had been waiting for.

"Hi, Sean, I have to make this quick. When you get to the hotel, there will be a box at the front desk for you, and it should give you all the information that you need. Sean, I'm just sorry that I didn't step up earlier and stop them from trying to railroad you, but hopefully you will find something in that box that will help you."

Sean said, "Thank you. I appreciate the help."

He got in line and boarded the plane headed to Michigan.

————

After Sean landed, he went and picked up his rental. Before he went to the hotel, he decided that he would go put flowers on his mother's, grandmother's, and Karen's graves. He stopped at Colemans —

every time he passed by the yellow building, it was a reminder of the good times that he spent with his mother. Every spring, they would go to Colemans to pick flowers to plant in their yard. This was before his mother became addicted to painkillers, and he moved in with his grandmother.

Sean's mom lost her fight with addiction when he was 15. He came to visit her one day, and she was lying on the living room floor with a bottle of oxycodone next to her. They were able to get her to the hospital, but she was gone within an hour. Sean sat in the room with her and watched her take her last breath.

He began to blink, holding back tears, thinking about losing three women who meant so much to him. They were the reasons he was the man that he was, and it hurt so badly every time he came home because it was a stinging reminder that they were no longer there.

After leaving the cemetery, Sean drove past his old high school Willow Run, the home of the Flyers. It was so hard to remember the good times because all he could think about was the horrible night that Karen was taken from him.

He drove past the school, but then he stopped, turned around and pulled into the parking lot; he parked in the same spot he did the night of prom. He stepped out of the car and looked at the two-story, brown, brick building. There were close to 600 students at the school when he attended. The community was very tight knit; that was, until the murder of Karen. After the murder, there were those who believed that Sean was the murderer and those who did not, and it caused a divide. Many people were scared because they believed that there was still a murderer on the loose.

Sean's knees felt weak as he began to walk around to the back of the school where he found Karen ten years ago. When he turned the corner, he spotted a familiar face. Standing there, was a woman with long, brown hair and even longer legs. She was wearing a black business suit that was perfectly tailored to her body.

When Sean approached her, a smile covered her face from ear to ear. Running toward Sean in her heels, she threw her arms around him and said, "Sean, I can't believe it's you. I haven't seen you since we graduated from this place. I didn't think you would show up for this reunion since you didn't come to our fifth year reunion. How are you? Are you married? Do you have children?"

Sean said, "It's nice to see you too, Courtney. It has been a long time. To be honest, I didn't know it was our reunion. I'm here to take care of family business. Maybe I will drop in to see everyone there and I'll answer all of your questions then; it will give us something to talk about."

Laughing, Courtney said, "I guess I did ambush you with questions. Does anyone else know that you are here?"

"No, and I would like to keep it that way. I have to get going, but when I saw you standing out here, I had to stop. It was nice seeing you...have a good day!"

Courtney reached out, grabbed Sean's arm, and said, "You know, I am really sorry about what happened to you after Karen's death."

Sean interrupted, "Karen's murder!"

"Right, her murder...I wish that things had gone differently. I always knew that you didn't have anything to with it, and I hated to see how the town turned on you."

"Courtney, like everyone else, you also turned your back on me when I needed you the most, but I understand, and I forgive you. There was a lot of pressure that everyone put on all of you. I just wished that my grandmother didn't have to witness it. Having to hear the rumors and to see the same kids that would come to her house to eat and hang out turn their backs on her grandson."

Looking down towards the ground, Courtney said, "Sean, I am so sorry. I really am."

Sean replied, "Can I ask you one question about the day that Karen was murdered?"

Repeatedly batting her long lashes, she replied, "Yes, ask me anything."

"Jordan told me that you guys got into a heated argument about Karen?"

Courtney's face went cold, and she shifted from one leg to the other. Pointing her finger at Sean, she yelled, "You know why!!"

"I don't!! Jordan never told me why. The day of prom you came over upset and crying, but all you said was Karen was the reason you couldn't go to prom" Sean protested.

"Karen told you!! She told me that she was going to tell you. I thought you knew, Sean."

"Thought I knew what? Karen never told me she spoke to you that day."

Exhaling Courtney said, "Chanda caught Karen and Jordan kissing against his car. When Karen saw Chanda, she slapped Jordan like she didn't initiate it. I always knew that she had a thing for him. When I called Jordan about it, he said that Karen came on to him, and I believed him. I still wanted to go to the dance with him, and I would have if I wasn't grounded because of Karen."

Sean said, "No wonder Karen didn't want Jordan to ride with us! Look I didn't mean to upset you, Courtney. Please keep my being here a secret."

Courtney nodded and walked away.

Sean never knew why Karen didn't want Jordan to ride with them to the dance; she was killed before she had a chance to tell him. If Jordan forced himself on her, he would have a good reason to silence her. Jordan needed Karen to keep her mouth shut about what he did to her.

6

COURTNEY COLLINS PROM DAY 2003...

"Jordan, I hate you! Chanda told me everything. She told me she saw you kissing Karen. How could you do this to me?"

Before Jordan could respond, I grabbed my brother's Louisville slugger from the garage and chased Jordan with it. He ran to the passenger side of his dad's blue car. I headed to the front of the car; he was not going to get away with cheating on me. Like the coward he is, he ran around to the back of the car.

I am so angry, but I have a big smile on my face. My therapist said it's the way I deal with stressful situations. Some people cry, others laugh, I smile. If I can't catch him, I'll hit the next best thing: his dad's car. Playing softball for 4 years is about to pay off...I spread my feet apart, leaned forward a little, pulled the bat back by my ear and swung as hard as I could; glass fell to the ground. I went to the other headlight and did the same thing.

Jordan ran to the front of the car. He looked down and then back up at me. He has never hit me before, but he looked like he was ready to, so I continued holding the bat...ready to swing again, if necessary.

Jordan yelled, "What is wrong with you? Are you crazy? My dad is going to kill me!"

"What's wrong with me??" I took the bat and hit the hood of the car. Then said, "This is your fault! Yours and Karen's! You think I damaged your car? Wait until I get my hands on Karen!"

My mom pulled into the driveway in her black Cadillac truck; she hopped out the car, and her black cat-eyed glasses fell to the ground. She felt around for them because she couldn't see without them. She yelled, "Courtney!! What is going on, what happened?"

I dropped the bat and ran over to her and said, "Jordan cheated on me with Karen. I was so upset. I...I...kind of took the bat, broke the headlights on his car and put a dent in his hood. He deserved it! How could he do this to me?"

Throwing her hands up in the air, she said, "Go into the house right now! Jordan, have your father call me...we will make sure the damage on the car is paid for. You may want to see if Karen is available to go with you to prom tonight because Courtney will not be going!" She turned her head and went into the house.

I stormed up the stairs into my room and slammed the door. On my closet, hung my beautiful, black and silver prom dress. My father was against buying something so expensive that would only be worn one time, but my mother told me to pick whatever dress I wanted. I began pacing back and forth. Becoming more enraged, I grabbed the pair of scissors from my desk and started plunging it into the dress, dragging it down to rip it. I did it over and over again as I screamed, *Karen, I am going to kill you!!*

My mother came into my room and took the scissors out of my hand.

"Courtney, your dress!! Have you lost your mind?"

I ran out of my room and took my mom's car keys off of the coffee table. I already can't go to prom, what else can they do to me? I got into her car and sped off, heading to Sean's grandmother's house.

After I returned home, I called Chanda to tell her everything that happened. At first, she didn't answer, which was strange to me because Chanda always answers my calls. She finally called back, and I told her that when I caught up with Karen, I was going to make her pay for what she had done.

7

Courtney paced the room waiting for her husband to come back from visiting his father. She knew that he would be upset to know that Sean was there, and that he was asking questions about the day Karen was murdered.

The hotel door opened, and Courtney's husband walked in. He was barely 5'5" and a little chunky. He wore a blue blazer and brown dress pants. Courtney had never been attracted to him physically, but what he lacked in looks, he more than made up with his finances.

"Hey, Court", Montel Kingsley said.

Throwing her hands in the air, Courtney said, "Montel, didn't you see my message to call me?"

"Yes, I saw it, but I was with my father talking business...and when I finished, I forgot to call you."

"Guess who I ran into at the school today?"

"Who?"

"Sean McKnight!"

Montel's smile turned into a frown. Curling his lips he said, "Sean? What made him show his face at this reunion? I thought he hated all of us...why would he want to see any of us?"

Walking towards Montel, Courtney said, "He claimed he didn't know about the reunion, and that he is here to take care of some family business. He is a detective now; do you think he knows something about Karen's murder?"

Sneering, Montel replied, "I'm still not so convinced that he is innocent, but I promise you, if he came to cause trouble, he is going to find it."

Courtney kissed Montel on his forehead and said, "I'm about to go get into the shower. You are taking me out for dinner and drinks. I think we both need to just unwind before the first day of the reunion tomorrow."

"That sounds good to me."

Courtney walked into the bathroom and cut on the shower. Montel got up, walked towards the bathroom and waited until he heard Courtney singing. Then, he grabbed his cell phone out of his blue blazer and walked out of the room.

"Jordan, we need to talk. I'm about to take Courtney out for dinner and drinks. When I get back, I'll call you so we can meet in the lobby of the hotel. Sean's here, and he may show up at the reunion; he is asking questions about Karen."

Jordan replied, "Ok, sounds like trouble to me. I'll see you tonight."

Montel walked back into the room before Courtney was out of the bathroom, he laid back on the bed with his arms folded behind his head. He wanted to talk to Jordan without Courtney around.

It had nothing to do with the fact that Jordan and Courtney were high school sweethearts. Montel knew that Courtney loved money, he had it, and Jordan did not. He needed the meeting with Jordan to be a secret. It wouldn't be hard to meet with him alone. Courtney often overindulged in wine, and Montel was sure that she would be fast asleep soon after they got back to the hotel.

8

MONTEL KINGSLEY PROM DAY
2003...

"Chanda, calm down, my father has it all under control."

Chanda cried out, "Montel, you don't understand if this gets out. I will never get into any of the colleges I applied to, and I'll lose the scholarships that I'm being offered...not to mention, we will be in serious legal trouble. I don't come from a rich family like you. This can ruin my whole future. You told me that nobody knew. I didn't tell anyone, so how did Karen find out?"

Montel exhaled, "Chanda, I said everything is under control. I am going to go and talk to Karen. She is one of my best friends; she would never say anything. I need you to stay calm...go get yourself ready for prom. The limo will be there to pick you up at 7:00pm."

Looking at her phone, Chanda said, "I'll be ready. Courtney keeps calling me. I can't deal with any of her drama right now. I'll call her back later. Look, Montel, you better handle Karen. I will not let her ruin my life!!"

I talked to Karen in confidence. I never thought that she would betray me. I went down into my father's office and told him I had to go out to grab a few things for prom. He told me that he would handle everything and to stay as far away from it as possible, but how could I not go talk to Karen?

I got into my yellow mustang, that my father bought for me when I turned 16. It caused a huge fight between him and grandfather. My grandfather believed that you should earn everything you receive, and things should not just be given to you. He never gave my dad anything; my dad had to work for the company starting off as an errand boy. I'm happy my father is different; if I ask for it, I get it.

I rolled my windows down and turned up the radio. I looked at my blackberry to see if I had any calls, and then I started to drive as fast as I could down the road. There was one truck driving slowly, so I sped around it. I looked in my rearview mirror and lights were flashing, and a siren turned on. I pulled over and the police car pulled up behind me. The officer approached my window and asked me if I knew why he was pulling me over.

This is the third time I have been pulled over this year for speeding. I did like my dad's lawyer told me and said, "No, I don't know why," and the officer asked for my license and registration.

Fifteen minutes later, the officer came back to my car, handed me my information back and said, "Okay, Mr. Kingsley, I was told to let you off with a warning. You were driving 20 miles over the speed limit. Slow down before you kill yourself or someone else."

With a smile on my face I replied, "Thank you officer."

I pulled in front of Karen's house, and her mom, who is just as beautiful as Karen, was outside working in the yard. She told me she would go get Karen for me; and when she came outside, Karen looked upset.

She walked over to me and said, "Why are you here? I guess you talked to Chanda. I know I told you I wouldn't say anything, but what you guys did was wrong, and it was not fair to others."

Before I knew it, I grabbed Karen by the arm and pulled her

towards me. Karen's neighbor, Ms. Mary, who was looking out her window, walked outside and yelled, "You get your hands off that girl!!"

I took off running to my car. I looked back in my rearview mirror, and that nosey, old

neighbor was talking to Karen...I put my foot on the gas and sped off.

9

Sean made it to the Marriot. When he walked in, there was a little boy, no older than two years old with a pacifier in his mouth and a tiny smile peeking out each side, running around the lobby. The boy's mother was running close behind him, apologizing to the guests as her son bumped into them.

That made Sean smile. He thought about Christopher, and how he would rather be home with him and Shelia instead of being in Michigan. Carrying a suitcase and a suit bag, Sean waited in line to check in.

A young lady with green hair, black lipstick, and face piercings waved for Sean to come up to the front desk.

"Name?"

"Sean McKnight."

Typing his name in she said, "I need your ID and a credit card to put on file."

Sean pulled out his beat-up, brown, leather wallet that Shelia gave him for their 1-year anniversary, grabbed his ID and credit card and handed them to the young lady.

Sean said, "I should have a package here at the desk."

Looking behind her she said, "Yeah, it's here...you may want to grab a bell cart because the box is heavy."

Sean went to the front door, grabbed a bell cart and went back to the front desk. He got his ID and credit card back, and he put the box and his luggage on the cart and headed towards the elevator.

Sean could not wait to get to the room and dig into the contents of the box. He walked down the hall pushing the cart, looking at the burgundy, gray, and cream swirls on the carpet. He stopped, pulled out his room key, stuck it into the door and entered.

Even though he missed Shelia, he was looking forward to having a king-sized bed all to himself for the weekend. He took the box and sat it on the table in front of the TV. He unbuttoned his shirt, rolled up his sleeves and began to pull folders out of the box. Sean decided that he probably should call Shelia before he fell down the rabbit hole of the contents. She was already upset with him for going; he didn't want to make things worse by not checking in.

"Hey, Sweetheart."

"Hi, Sean, I miss you already."

"I miss you too! What are you and Chris doing?"

"I'm cleaning up spilled milk, and he is currently about to jump off the couch."

Sean heard a thump and then a cry.

Shelia exclaimed, "I have to get off the phone...Chris just hit his leg on the table. I'll call you back after I put him to bed."

Shelia hung up and Sean went back to his box. It was so much to go through, but he was up for the task. He was hungry, so he ordered room service...a steak and potatoes. He went over to the coffee machine and began to brew a pot. He was going to need all the caffeine he could get.

Sean pulled out a picture, and it was of the crime scene. He had not seen it since he was interrogated by Detective Montgomery. His heart began to race, and as tears built up in his eyes, he began to cry.

He threw the photo across the room and yelled, "WHY? WHY? Why did this happen to you, Karen? I am so sorry I was not outside to protect you. I give you my word that soon this will all be over, and your case will be solved, just like I promised you."

Sean reached over and pulled some tissue out of the box on the counter. He wiped his eyes and nose, walked back over to the box and opened a folder labeled "Witnesses."

He flipped through some statements; most of them he had read before, but there was one that he hadn't seen. It was not with the official statements. This note was handwritten by Detective Montgomery. It read: *MH (unreliable witness) friend of suspect's grandmother.*

Sean knew that it had to be referring to Ms. Mary Hall. He had known her his entire life. She had been his grandmother's best friend since childhood. Ms. Mary is what everyone called her. She moved from Alabama to Ypsilanti, and Sean's grandparents moved to the neighborhood shortly after.

Ms. Mary was one of the first black mail carriers in the area. She was 6 feet tall and when she was not at work, she sat on her porch in her rocking chair, with her shotgun leaned up against the house. She always had her flask filled with whiskey and was known for her knowledge and love of cigars.

A lot of the black women in the 1950s looked to her for protection, since the police were not in a hurry to protect those in the black neighborhoods. She sent a couple of men to the hospital, and they were too afraid of Ms. Mary to dare say that she was the one who put them there.

Ms. Mary lived right across the street from Karen. In fact, that is how Sean became interested in Karen. He would go over to Ms. Mary's with his grandmother, and while they would gossip, he would go across the street and sit on Karen's porch, and they would talk for hours.

Sean decided that he would go to visit Ms. Mary in the morning. There was a knock on his door, and a bubbly young lady pushed in a cart with a white cloth draped across it. It had three plates covered with a silver top, a glass of water, and a napkin that tightly held his silverware. He handed her a crispy $20 bill for a tip. She thanked him and walked out of the room.

10

Jordan walked into the hotel lobby and made his way to the bar. Montel was working on his second Martini, as he got up and waved Jordan over to him. Jordan walked over and sat down in his leather motorcycle pants and vest. He was one of the only ones from the high school clique who still lived in town.

Jordan had a scholarship to play basketball at U of M, but he tore his ACL playing pick-up basketball the summer before he was to start college. He had surgery and was never the same; and he eventually lost his scholarship.

He started drinking heavily soon after. Everyone thought that he would be playing in the NBA right now. He now owns an auto repair shop in Ypsilanti and coaches the varsity boys' basketball team at Willow Run High School.

"Jordan, my man!" Montel said with a smile.

"Hi, my brother, it's good to see you." Jordan replied, as he reached out to hug Montel.

"How is everything going with your shop and the basketball team? Be looking out for a check from the Kingsley corporation at the end of the month. I'm sure you could use it for some new jerseys or equipment."

"Thank you! Your donations are appreciated! Last summer we were able to pay for all the boys to go to camp," Jordan said excitedly.

"Good, good...I'm going to need something from you. Can you find out why Sean is here and asking questions about Karen? The last time he saw us, he told us he hated us and never wanted to see any of us again... and now he is back in town. He told Court he wasn't here for the reunion, but he may show-up, which of course means trouble."

Looking around at the empty room, Jordan said, "Maybe he just changed his mind and wanted to see everyone."

Montel took a sip of his martini and said, "No, I have a feeling Sean is here for trouble. I know that he won't talk to me, but maybe he will talk to you. You guys were best friends for a long time."

Staring down at the floor, Jordan said, "Some best friend I was. When Sean needed me most, I sided with everyone against him. I don't think he will talk to me, but I'll try."

Montel replied, "Thank you, and I will email the accountant to make sure that the check was sent out to you."

"Do you know what hotel he is staying at?"

Tapping his finger on the bar Montel said, "No, but I have someone who can find out for us. I will contact him, and as soon as I know something, I'll give you a call."

"Sounds good, I'll be waiting."

Jordan began to walk back to his motorcycle. He thought about all he and Sean had been through together. When Jordan's dad would beat on his mother, Sean's grandmother would always let Jordan come over and spend the night. Most of the time, that stopped Jordan from getting a beating. They would stay up all night playing video games in hopes that they could escape the realities of their lives.

Jordan and Sean had big dreams of going to U of M and playing basketball, then going to the NBA together. They both dreamed of playing for the Detroit Pistons. Sean's scholarship was revoked when he became a suspect in Karen's murder. He tried to fight it, but the school used the morality clause in the contract he signed against him. Detective Montgomery made sure that they had all the evidence they needed to make their decision.

Jordan really didn't want to get information for Montel, but he felt that he owed him. When his auto shop was being foreclosed on, it was Montel and Courtney who gave him the money to save his business.

Jordan always believed it was more Courtney than Montel. Even though they broke up right after high school, Courtney still had a soft spot for Jordan, and he was still in love with her. Deep down, Jordan wished that Courtney had come downstairs so he could have seen her.

As Jordan straddled his motorcycle, his phone buzzed...it was Montel.

"He is staying at the Eagle Crest Marriot on S. Huron Street."

Jordan exhaled, "That was fast. How did you find that out?"

"Let's just say my dad has the right people working for us."

Jordan said, "Would you happen to have a room number?"

"No, but when you go, ask for Naomi, she is going to call him and ask him to come down to the front desk. Call me tonight after you talk to him. I'll be waiting."

———

Sean received a call from the receptionist, and he rushed downstairs. There was only one person who knew what hotel he was staying at, and they decided not to meet up because they didn't want to be seen together. It must have been important; maybe it was some new evidence.

Sean could not believe his eyes when he walked into the hotel lobby. It was Jordan Kimmble. Sean hadn't seen him since he left Michigan...his heart raced. He wanted to run across the lobby and punch Jordan in the face, especially since his conversation with Courtney earlier, when he found out what Jordan had done to Karen.

Sean knew that he had to keep his cool so that he didn't blow everything.

Jordan had a big smile on his face. He was so happy to see Sean; he started to walk across the lobby.

"What's up, Sean?" Jordan said, as he pulled Sean towards him with one hand, while patting his shoulder with the other.

Pushing away, Sean replied, "What's up?"

"Look at you, all buffed...you are not the scrawny kid that I knew! I hear that you are a big-time detective now," scoffed Jordan.

Laughing, Sean said, "I'm the detective, but you found me. You must have heard I was here from Courtney or Montel. I'm curious as to how you found out what hotel I'm staying at?"

"Montel told me. Court must have told him."

Sean decided not to call Jordan out on the lie. He never told Courtney where he was staying. Instead, he decided to play along and see what information he could get from Jordan.

Sean said, "Why don't we go have a seat at the bar and catch up."

Elated, Jordan said, "I could use a night cap."

They sat down at the end of the bar so that they would be away from the other guests. Throwing the white towel over his shoulder while twirling a toothpick around in his mouth, the bartender walks over to them and said, "This is last call...what will it be?"

Sean said, "I'll have a Corona."

Jordan said, "Rum and Coke."

"You look good, Sean. You haven't aged a bit. I can't believe that you, out of all people, became a cop."

Shaking his head in agreement, Sean said, "Well, we never know what curveball life will throw at us, or how we would react! You, of all people, should know that. When basketball was not an option anymore, I took up criminology in school. I decided to become a police officer to protect people like me and get justice for people like Karen. I hear that you own an auto repair shop."

Sighing, Jordan said, "Yeah, and I coach the varsity boys' basketball team at our old high school."

"Go Flyers!" Sean chanted.

The bartender sat the drinks on the bar, and Jordan took a big gulp, closing his eyes tightly as he swallowed. Sitting his glass down, he said, "Sean, I'm sorry. I know it doesn't mean much now, but I am very sorry for abandoning you when you needed me the most."

"You're right...it doesn't mean much now." He replied with cold, dark eyes.

Jordan raised his voice and said, "Sean, why are you here?"

The couple holding hands at the end of the bar looked up, aggravated by Jordan's outburst. They got up and moved to a table in the lobby.

Jordan said, "Look, I didn't mean to yell, but if you hate us all so much, why did you come to the reunion...and why are you asking questions about Karen?"

Sean said, "Who said I was here for the reunion? I'm here to handle some business. I finally decided to sell grandma's home. I am supposed to meet up with some realtors. I didn't even know about the reunion until I saw Courtney earlier today."

Sean picked up his beer and took a sip, waiting for Jordan's reply. He could tell that he had thrown him off guard.

"Well, why were you asking about Karen?"

"Curiosity." Sean replied.

Taking another sip from his Corona, Sean said, "Since we are on the subject of Karen. What happened between you two the night of prom? She was adamant that she did not want you to ride with us, and then she told me she had something to tell me, but she never got the chance."

Jordan began to cough; his eyes began to water, and he started to scratch his neck.

Sean exclaimed, "Jordan, did that question make you nervous?"

"No, I just hate thinking about that day, that's all."

"So...What happened?"

Jordan stood up and said, "Thanks for the drink, old friend. You have a nice night."

Sean watched as Jordan walked away. He hoped that Jordan would go report back to whoever sent him, and that it would ease their suspicion. He needed them oblivious to his real reason for being there.

Sean walked up to the front desk and said, "I don't want any more interruptions. If anyone else comes, tell them that I'm not available. He gave the receptionist $20 and went back to his room."

Sean lay back on the bed. He grabbed the phone and called Shelia to tell her good night. He stared at the ceiling for hours; he knew that someone had sent Jordan there, and it had to be someone with pull to be able to find out where he was staying. He suspected it was Montel Kingsley.

Sean flopped from one side of the bed to the other. He wrapped his arms around the pillow, hoping that he could trick himself into thinking he was holding Shelia. His mind was racing a mile a minute, and he could not slow it down so that he could relax to sleep. *Why would Montel be so concerned that I'm here, that he would send Jordan to interrogate me.* Sean turned the TV on and watched it until he finally fell fast asleep.

11

JORDAN KIMMBLE PROM DAY
2003...

"I hate you, Jordan, and I am going to tell Sean everything!" Karen yelled.

"Karen, you were flirting with me...I just followed your lead."

"How is me yelling, "STOP!" and telling you, "NO," flirting? What if Chanda had not come over when she did? I can't believe you told her that I started kissing you. I hate you!" Karen yelled as she hung up the phone.

I asked Chanda not to say anything to Courtney about what she saw, but they were best friends, and I knew that my request was unreasonable. The only thing on my mind was getting to Courtney's and then talking to Sean to try to convince him into believing that Karen came on to me.

My dad was passed out on the couch. He had come home drunk at 2:00am, and my mother locked the bedroom door so that he could not get in. It was usually on these nights he would come home drunk and hit my mom. Then I would try to protect my mom and he would hit me. He must be too tired to fight tonight.

I tiptoed towards my dad and took the keys to his car out of his blue, grease-stained work jacket. He has been doing the same job as an auto mechanic for the last 20 years. I can't wait to get away from him. In a few more months, I'll be at U of M playing basketball. I'm going to go to the NBA and move my mom far away from that monster. I looked at my phone; I had 25 missed calls from Courtney.

I know how much Courtney hates Karen, so I'll just convince her that Karen was flirting with me, and she kissed me.

When I pulled up to Courtney's house, she was sitting on the porch with the phone in her hand crying. I got out and she dropped the phone. Then, she picked up her brother's bat and started hitting my dad's car.

She screamed, "This is what I am going to do to that snake's head when I get my hands on her. How could you do this to me, Jordan?"

I slowly walked towards Courtney. She was still holding the bat and was ready to swing. I was mad enough to punch her, but I would never be like my dad and put my hands on anyone I loved. Courtney's mom pulled up, ordered Courtney into the house and informed me that I would be going to prom alone.

I looked at my dad's car in disbelief: two broken headlights and dents on the hood. He is going to beat me for sure. My dad is working midnights this week; he had a shop full of cars that had to be fixed. He should be sleeping and not see the car until after I go to prom. I have to make sure Karen doesn't tell Sean anything. I will probably need somewhere to stay after my dad sees his car, and Sean's grandmother's house has been my refuge over the years.

I need to call Sean; I'm sure Karen has not said anything yet. Sean would have already been over to my house to beat me up. My body began to overheat as I dialed Sean's number.

"Hey, Jordan!! I am so excited about tonight."

"I have bad news; Courtney is grounded and can't go to prom, so I don't know if I'm going."

"What!!" Sean exclaimed. "What did she do?"

"She went psycho and started to beat my dad's car with a bat."

"Why would she do that?" Sean exclaimed.

"I don't know. When I pulled into her driveway, she started swinging."

Sean protested, "You should still go. You can ride with me and Karen. I'm sure she won't mind."

I said, "No, it's ok."

Sean replied, "I won't take 'no' for an answer. Look, this is Karen calling me now. I'll call you back."

Before I could say anything, else Sean hung up. I was sure that Karen was telling him everything. Maybe not telling Sean my side of the story first was a mistake. One thing I know for certain is if Sean comes swinging a bat, he will be going for my head not the car. Sean was small, but he was strong. I watched him beat up one of his mom's boyfriends after they got evicted because the boyfriend was using their rent money to buy drugs.

My phone began to ring; it's Sean...*Oh no! Did Karen tell him?* My hands won't stop shaking as I pick up the phone. "What's up, Sean?" I whispered.

"I have some bad news, man. Karen doesn't want you to ride with us to prom. I'm not sure why. I'm sorry."

I breathed an air of relief. Pretending to be upset, I said, "You just told me I could ride with you all. You know what, Sean? Never mind, I'll figure it out...see you tonight."

12

S ean began to squint and was awoken by the sun shining through the cracks of the blinds. He looked at his watch and jumped out of bed. It was 9:00am...he had overslept. He wanted to look over some more of the files before he left to visit Ms. Mary. He put on his blue jeans, polo shirt, and Detroit Tigers baseball cap and went downstairs to grab some breakfast.

He walked past the bagels, which he usually ate every morning at home and went over to the tall chef with the big mustache, that was perfectly curled on each side, and ordered a veggie omelet. Sean spotted a seat in the corner where he could have some privacy to eat and look over some more of the detective's notes. He looked outside at the blue, clear sky — the sun reflecting off the window gently warmed his face.

Sean had seen the official witnesses' statements a thousand times. He was more interested in the written notes and the things that were not included. Sean looked up at the television on the wall and the local news was on. To his surprise, there was Craig Kingsley, the CEO of the Kingsley Corp. What was more interesting to Sean, was the man standing in front of Mr. Kingsley, with black sunglasses on and his arm folded.

He was 6 foot tall with salt and pepper hair and was wearing a black, tailored suit. Sean would never forget that face. It was Detective Landen Montgomery. Sean walked over to the TV to hear what the newscasters were saying. Across the bottom of the TV, it said *Philanthropist and Ypsilanti Native Gives Back to the Community.* The Kingsley Corp was building a community center. It would have a gym and an indoor swimming pool. During the school year, they would offer an after-school program.

Sean now knew his suspicions were correct. It was Detective Montgomery who found out where he was staying. Sean decided not to take any chances and went back upstairs, grabbed the box of evidence and brought it with him. He would not put it past them to snoop through his room while he was out.

On his way to Ms. Mary's house, Sean decided that he would take Tony up on his offer to help. He pulled over and grabbed his cell phone that slid on the floor after he merged onto the expressway and called Tony.

"Hey, Tony."

"Hey, Sean, how is everything going?"

"Well, I had an unexpected visitor last night, and I just saw something interesting on the local news. Can you see what you can find out about Detective Landen Montgomery, with regards to the Kingsley corporation?"

Tony Exclaimed, "Will do, I'll call you as soon as I have some information for you."

———

Sean pulled onto the street in front of Ms. Mary's house. He remembered that she did not allow anyone to pull into her driveway. The house seemed a lot smaller than it did when he was growing up. He opened the rusted gate and walked up to the front porch. In the window, was a black and red sign that said, "No Tres-passing."

The door was opened, and through the screen, sitting on a brown recliner facing Sean, was Ms. Mary.

He said, "Ms. Mary, it's me, Sean McKnight. I wanted to say hello and ask you a few questions, if you are up to it." Sean made sure that he announced himself quickly because Ms. Mary was quick to pull out her gun.

A frail lady, with gray hair and a tube in her nose pulling an oxygen tank behind her, opened the door. Sean barely recognized Ms. Mary. He was used to seeing a strong, feisty, healthy woman, who selflessly helped everyone she could in the neighborhood.

"Sean! Well, aren't you a sight for sore eyes? If you don't get your behind in here! I haven't seen you since we buried my dearest friend, your grandmother. You know I go to visit her every Friday. Push all that mail to the side and have a seat. You remember when you and your grandmother used to come here every Friday, and we would play cards, drink, and of course gossip? I miss those days; you would go across the street and sit and talk to that poor young girl who was murdered. You know they never found her killer? It broke my heart and your grandmother's the way they tried to pin that on you."

Grabbing her hand, Sean said, "Yes, ma'am, I do remember. Those were some good times. My favorite part was coming over and eating catfish and grits. I love your catfish."

With watery eyes, Ms. Mary said, "Well, this may be the last time that you see me, Son. You see, I was diagnosed with a rare and aggressive form of cancer, and they gave me less than 6 months to live. I'm at peace with it; my husband, son, and best friend are no longer here. You know this world can be a lonely place, and some-times that loneliest can feel like a death sentence."

In a whisper, Sean sad, "I'm so sorry, Ms. Mary." He wrapped his arms around her, laying his head on her shoulder. She patted his back and said, "Sean, would you like something to drink?"

"No, ma'am, I'm fine."

"Well, would you mind grabbing me a beer?"

Smiling, Sean went into the kitchen and grabbed a cold Bud Light out of the fridge. Being in the kitchen was like going back in time, she still had the same orange and brown flowered wallpaper. He looked at the kitchen table that had a white lace doily draped over it. In the middle of the table, was a stack of blue envelopes, and on the very top, was a paper with the Kingsley Corp letterhead on it. Sean saw two other blue envelopes like that sitting on the couch next to him in the living room.

Walking back into the living room, Sean said, "Ms. Mary, do you remember when Karen was murdered and being questioned by Detective Montgomery?"

Sitting her beer down, Ms. Mary said, "I sure do remember that buffoon. He dismissed everything I said, and he tried to make it seem like I was making up a story to help you out. I told him that I may be a lot of things, but a liar ain't one of them! And then I kicked him out of my house. It seemed like his scrawny partner wanted to hear more, but Detective Montgomery kept shutting him down too."

Ms. Mary grabbed her handkerchief and began to cough in it. Sean watched helplessly, as the once strong woman that he knew struggled for every breath.

Sean said, "Ms. Mary, do you need me to come back? Is this too much for you right now?"

Wagging her finger at him, she said, "Don't be silly. I haven't had a guest in a few weeks. I'm not about to let a little coughing run you off. Now what is your question for me, Son?"

"What did you tell the detectives that you saw that day?"

"I told them that I saw a young man arguing with Karen the night that she was murdered. I told him that I did not see his face, but the boy was very angry, and he had her pinned up on the fence, gripping her arm tightly until I ran him off. The buffoon asked me if it could be you, and I told him NO. He was at least 3 inches shorter than you, and he was a little chubby. I went out on the porch and yelled that if he didn't let her go, I would pull out my shotgun, and he ran and jumped into a yellow car."

"Do you remember anything else about him?"

"No, Son, that's all."

Sean glanced down, looking at the mail on the couch. Even though he knew it was none of his business, he was curious as to why she had received mail from the Kingsley Corp.

He said, "Ms. Mary, I noticed when I was grabbing your beer that you had letters from the Kingsley Corp, and I see that you have a few more unopened letters sitting here on the couch from them."

Abruptly, she replied, "Those rascals are trying to buy us all out of our homes so they can build another one of their plants here. I saw this morning that they are building a new community center. They are not fooling me; they are doing it to gain the support of the community. A lot of folks have sold to them, but I won't, and I have told them as much several times. Those letters are new offers that they've sent. Every time they send a new letter, they offer me more money than the last. It ain't enough money in the world for me to sell my land to that snake, Craig Kingsley. He is just as horrible as his father, Mathis Kingsley. You know your grandma worked for them when she and your grandfather first moved to Ypsilanti. Your grandmother and others in the neighborhood would say with the way Mathis treated black folks, he must have thought that the south had won."

Sean walked over and gave Ms. Mary a kiss on the cheek and said, "Ms. Mary, thank you, you have helped me more than you know. I'm in town for a couple of days. How about I come by tomorrow afternoon, and we catch up some more?"

Rubbing the side of his face, she said, "I would love that, Sean. Before you go, I need to tell you something. You know your grandmother loved you very much...until the day she died, she bragged on you. When you became a police officer and then made detective, that's all she could talk about. Sean, you know your grandmother never believed that you killed that girl. She had you move with your aunt because she was afraid for you. Even though they dropped the charges against you, there were a lot of people, including the girl's family, who thought you were guilty. Well, I just thought you ought to know that. You call before you come, and I'll have some catfish and grits waiting."

Sean said, "Yes ma'am," as he walked out of the door with tears streaming down his face.

13

Sean needed to hear that. He knew that his grandmother loved him, and even though she reassured him over and over again that she believed him, there was a part of him that wasn't very sure.

Sean sat in his car thinking about all that Ms. Mary had told him. He could think of one chubby boy that was a couple of inches smaller than him when they were in school, and he drove a yellow mustang, and that was Montel Kingsley. Nowhere in Montel's statement to the police did he mention that he had seen Karen earlier that day, and he definitely did not mention them getting into an argument.

Sean began digging into the files and pulled out Montel's statement to read it over again:

"I went to pick up my date, Chanda Powers, for prom. She came outside and was upset. I asked her what was wrong...she said that Karen had ruined the whole night; because of her, Courtney couldn't go to the dance. I told Chanda that it was not Karen's fault that Courtney lost her temper and smashed up Jordan's car.

Chanda said if Karen hadn't done what she did, then Courtney would have never had reacted that way. I asked Chanda what Karen had done, and she said that I would find out at the dance because she was going to expose Karen, and that Sean would be very upset when he found out. I told Chanda that it was not a good idea, but she said she was going to do it anyway.

When we were at the dance, I saw Jordan and Chanda arguing. I walked over to where they were and told Jordan to leave my date alone, because he was upsetting her. Jordan told me to mind my business and pushed me. I remember Sean grabbing me after Jordan punched me. The hall monitor, Paul Stewart, ran over, grabbed Jordan and pushed him away from me. I saw Karen jerk her arm away from Sean, and then she ran out of the auditorium, with Sean running after her. Maybe 10 minutes later, I saw a group of people running outside, and I followed. When I got out there, I saw Sean kneeling beside Karen, who was in a pool of blood."

Sean sat the statement on the passenger seat and leaned his head against the headrest. He never ran outside after Karen. It was right there in Paul Stewart's statement which said, *"I pulled Jordan off Montel and walked him out of the dance into the hallway so that he could calm down. We talked for a few minutes, and then Sean came into the hallway. I asked Sean what started the altercation, and he said he did not know. He asked me if I saw where Karen ran off to...I told him, 'No' and he ran off and continued looking for her. I saw him stop and talk to Chanda Powers, and then he ran outside. A few minutes later, I ran outside and thought I saw a red car pulling into the street from the parking lot, but there was so much commotion, I could be wrong. I walked over to the crowd, saw Sean holding Karen in his arms, and people were whispering that he killed her."*

That was not the only inconsistency in the witness statements. When Detective Montgomery brought the evidence to the district attorney, he told him that the small difference between stories was because the kids were in shock. The only evidence that they had against Sean was that Karen's blood was all over him, and that Montel and Chanda both said they saw Sean run outside behind Karen.

Detective Montgomery was adamant that Sean was the only one

with the means, opportunity, and motive. He came up with a story that Karen was breaking up with Sean, he found out, flew into an uncontrollable rage and killed her.

After Sean's grandmother hired an attorney, with the help of Ms. Mary, Sean's attorney brought evidence to the attention of district attorney that contradicted all the "evidence" that the police had. Besides Paul Stewart's statement, there was other evidence, like an imprint that was on Karen's face…it came from something like a ring, and it had to have happened after Karen ran out of the gym. There were a lot of pictures taken that day, and Karen did not have any marks on her face before or during the dance.

Karen was also wearing fake nails, and one of them was broken, which probably happened during the altercation with the murderer. The medical examiner said that the suspect would have scratches somewhere on their body. Sean had no scratches on him, which could be seen from the pictures that the police took of him. The other piece of evidence, that the detective didn't mention to the district attorney, was that the medical examiner believed that the murderer was most likely right-handed because of the stab wounds and because of where the mark from the impression on Karen's face was. Sean was left-handed.

None of the evidence that proved that Sean was innocent mattered to the people in the town. By the time his defense attorney was hired, and the evidence was presented to the district attorney, Sean was already guilty in the public eye, and Detective Montgomery made sure of that.

The charges were eventually dropped with the apologies of the district attorney, who said that Detective Montgomery and his partner's work was sloppy and egregious. Soon after, Detective Montgomery retired from the police force.

14

Sean could not stop thinking about his visit with Ms. Mary. He had planned to stay at the hotel and continue to look at the contents in the box, but then decided to join his classmates for the first day of the class reunion instead.

He wanted to use the information that he just learned from his visit to see if he could get a reaction out of anyone, particularly Montel Kingsley.

Sean had not heard back from Tony, so he picked up his phone and began calling him.

"I was just about to call you, Sean" Tony said.

"I'm sure you are sitting with your feet up eating your nasty burnt popcorn and drinking coffee," Sean said jokingly.

"You think you know me...actually, I'm eating burnt popcorn and drinking a Diet Coke. I'm trying cut down on my caffeine."

Holding back his laugh, Sean replied, "You cutting back on caffeine? Man, that's your lifeline...you know, Tony, Diet Coke has caffeine too."

Tony replied, "I know, I didn't say that I wasn't having any caffeine...I said cutting back. Anyway, enough about me and my caffeine. Let's talk about Detective Montgomery. I found out that for the last nine years he has been head of security for the Kingsley Corp.

The Kingsley Corp must be paying him very well. Detective Montgomery owns a home in Michigan and one in Florida, and he is the owner of a few luxury vehicles. He is one of the corporation's highest paid employees.

Sean, are you sure that you don't need me to come out there to watch your six? You are dealing with some pretty powerful characters."

Taking a deep breath, Sean said, "I appreciate you, brother, but I'm good. I need you in Rhode Island just in case Shelia needs anything."

"Okay, the offer stands, if you change your mind."

———

Sean knew that Tony was right; he had no idea who he was going up against. All Sean had was a bunch of pieces of a puzzle that he needed to put together, and time was running out. He pulled into the hotel parking lot and unfastened the first few buttons on his shirt. He put his hands behind his head and closed his eyes while taking a few deep breaths.

There was a knock on Sean's car window, and he jumped. His first reaction was to go for his gun. He looked over and it was the receptionist from the front desk at the hotel.

Sean rolled his window down and said, "Don't ever do that again. You scared me to death. You could have gotten yourself shot."

She replied, "Look, sorry if I scared you...I don't have a lot of time; I'm on my lunch break. There was a man here earlier asking about you; he said he was a friend and asked for your room number. He was a tall man, looked like he was in his late forty's, early fifties. He told me not to tell you, but nobody tells me what to do...besides, he seems like a jerk. He drove off in one of those black Town cars."

"Thank you...you didn't have to tell me. I appreciate it."

Smiling, she said, "Well, I have a soft spot for handsome men." She walked towards her car, looking back over her shoulder to see if Sean was looking.

Sean flashed a smile and waved. He began to look around, wondering if he was being watched. He grabbed the box, went inside and sat on the neatly made bed. He pulled out the itinerary on the invitation to the reunion that he was sent, but never replied to. The first day would be spent bowling and doing karaoke with his schoolmates.

Sean picked up the Marriot notepad that was sitting on the desk by his bed and wrote: *Kingsley Corp>Detective Montgomery>Montel Kingsley>Jordan Kimmble>Karen.* Sean was positive that he knew the players. Now, it was time for him to force them to play a card.

15

Some of Sean's best memories growing up was hanging with his friends at Ypsi-Arbor bowling alley. He thought about all the times that he and Jordan battled, both determined to prove that they were the better bowler. Not to mention the show they put on to impress the ladies. Even then, there was only one girl that Sean wanted to impress, and that was Karen.

Sean shook his head and began rubbing his eyebrows and reminiscing about the last time they all went bowling together as a group. Sean wore his red, Adidas, zip-up jogging suit with the matching red and white Adidas, and Jordan wore his matching green outfit.

He took a deep breath, pulled down the visor and looked at himself in the mirror. He rubbed his chin, running his fingers over stubble, which was a reminder that he needed to shave. He got out of the car and walked into the bowling alley. It was a different bowling alley than the one they hung out at as kids. Ypsi-Arbor had closed down, so they met at a different one in Westland. At the entrance, was an arch of red and white balloons and a banner attached that had "Willow Run Class of 2003" written on it.

Sean was greeted at the front by one of his former classmates. She had dark brown hair that was cut into a bob. She was a lot smaller than he remembered her being in school. He recognized her face, but he could not remember her name.

Looking down at guest list, she said, "Name?"

"Sean McKnight."

She looked up, smiled and said, "Oh my God, Sean! I haven't seen you since graduation. It's me Lauryn!! You remember we had science together in Mr. Gobel's class!!"

Smirking, Sean said, "How are you, Lauryn?"

She replied, "I'm fine...but Sean, you are not on the list. We already set the teams up with the list of people who RSVP'd."

"That's ok! I haven't seen my former classmates in a while. I am going to walk around and get reacquainted with everyone."

Lauryn hardly waited until Sean walked away before she started telling people that he was at the reunion. This would be the first time that his classmates had seen him since graduation. The ceremony was on a Saturday, and Sunday morning, Sean said goodbye to his grandmother and rode to Ohio to live with his aunt. She was not a biological aunt...she was best friends with Sean's mother.

He walked over to the bar, and his smile turned into a frown. He was overtaken by the smell of old beer and chicken wings. He quickly walked away and began scanning the room for his old clique, and over in the far corner, he spotted Jordan and Courtney.

While headed towards the lane, one of his former classmates wearing a red and white, 2003 Willow Run Flyer reunion t-shirt approached Sean and said, "Hey, I'm happy you are here! I don't know if you remember me, but you used to stand up for me when the other kids would tease me at school. Just so you know, I have a black belt now, so let me know if you need any assistance tonight." They laughed as Sean walked away.

He made it over to the lane, and Montel had a bowling ball in his hand and his arm stretched out ready to send it down the alley. Sean said, "How much you wanna bet it goes into the gutter?"

Montel, Jordan, Courtney, and Chanda all turn around. Chanda ran over to Sean and wrapped her arms around him, burying her face in his chest.

"Sean, it is so good to see you! Courtney told me you were in town. I'm so happy that you decided to come to the reunion."

Sean looked down at Chanda. She had not changed a bit. She had the prettiest smile that connected to the most beautiful dimples. He said, "It's good to see you, too."

Montel walked over towards Sean and said, "Sean, my man, what a surprise! It's good to see you."

Sean's eyebrows instantly lowered, and the smile that greeted Chanda turned into a frown. He said, "Montel, I am sure it is not a surprise. I saw your wife yesterday, and I am positive that Jordan reported back to you after our visit last night."

Smirking, Montel said, "Sean, why are you here?"

Courtney yelled, "Montel, it's your turn...come on and play!"

Throwing his index finger up towards Courtney, Montel replied, "No, Sean walked in here with a chip on his shoulder. He has made it perfectly clear that he hates us all, so I want to know why he is here."

Sean knew that Montel was trying to provoke him. He had to play it smart; he didn't want everyone's defenses up...he needed them all to be at ease, so that he could get the answers he came for.

Sean replied, "You are right. I was very angry when I left Ypsi to go to Ohio. I'm here in town to sell my grandmother's house. I ran into Courtney at the high school, and she told me about the reunion, so I thought that it was time to bury the hatchet."

Chanda said, "Go get some bowling shoes and join us...it will be like old times."

Sean replied, "I think I will."

Montel stomped back to the lane and rolled the ball... it effortlessly found its way down the gutter to the pit. A roar of laughter ensued, and then Courtney grabbed her purple bowling ball and walked up to the lane.

Sean was waiting in line to get his bowling shoes. He was

exhausted from the hugs and the fake similes that he gave out to former classmates as they walked up and reintroduced themselves to him. And he was embarrassed by the fact that he didn't remember a lot of them.

When he was approaching the counter, Montel walked up, threw money down and said, "I'll pay for his game."

Pushing the money back towards Montel, Sean replied, "No, thank you!"

Montel, clinching his jaws, said, "I insist. Besides I know you don't make that much money as a detective."

Facing Montel, Sean said, "I see you haven't changed a bit. You are still trying to buy your friends."

Sean handed the attendant his money, and the attendant plopped his size 11, red and black bowling shoes on the table. He held out his hand and Sean handed him one of his shoes and began to walk back towards the others. Montel walked quickly behind Sean and grabbed his shoulder. Sean, in turn, grabbed Montel's wrist and spun towards him, while twisting just enough for Montel to grimace.

Sean looked Montel in the eyes and said, "To answer your question. I am here to take care of family business, but I know what you did, and I will eventually make you, and anyone else involved in Karen's murder, pay."

Lauryn walked over and said, "Is everything ok?"

Sean said, "Montel is everything ok?" Montel nodded while pulling his wrist away from Sean.

Montel yelled, "Courtney, get our things. It is time to go."

Courtney said, "Montel, our game just started and I'm waiting for my drink."

Montel replied sharply, "Grab our things and let's go!"

Courtney looked towards the ground, grabbed her purse and headed towards Montel.

Montel walked by Sean and said, "You are going to regret coming here."

Sean laughed, as Montel reached for Courtney's hand, and she pulled away.

Chanda walked over to Sean and said, "What was that about?"

"Montel is still intimidated by my presence, I guess." They laughed and walked back to the lane.

————

After scoring a 200 on the last game and winning the best 2 out of 3, Sean left the bowling alley and headed to the hotel. As he was driving, he noticed bright lights quickly approaching his car. He sped up a little, but the car continued coming closer and closer. He glanced into the rearview mirror...the light was so bright, he had to squint. He was able to make out a black Town Car with tinted windows. The car resembled the description that the hotel receptionist had given him.

Sean stepped on his brakes a couple of times, hoping that the idiot would get the hint and back off some, but the driver came closer. Sean sped up, and the car followed suit.

Soon, Sean was going 50 MPH in a 25 MPH zone. The car that had been trailing him sped up beside him and began to come over into his lane in an attempt to run him off the road. Sean hit his brakes, and his car started to spin; he hit a patch of gravel and began to slide off the road towards a ditch. Sean quickly swerved to the left and ended up back on the road. The black car sped off. Sean looked to get a license plate number, but the plate was covered.

Sean's heart was racing. He had been in many close calls before in his years as a patrolman. He began to punch the steering wheel. Coming up quickly behind Sean, were more bright lights. He opened his glove compartment box and grabbed his gun just in case they were coming back. The car drove past and then stopped.

Sean stepped out of the car with his gun in his hand, it was a different car, but he didn't know if it was someone else coming to finish the job. Chanda Powers stepped out of the silver Prius. Sean stuck his gun in the front of his jeans and walked towards Chanda.

Running towards Sean, she said, "Sean, oh my God!! Are you ok? What happened?"

"Yes, I am fine. Someone just tried to run me off the road. I must have pissed somebody off."

"Maybe you should call the police?"

Sean said, "I am the police."

Walking back towards his car, Sean noticed it leaning on the passenger side...the tire was flat. He walked around to the back of the car and opened the trunk, pulling out a spare tire. He asked Chanda if she would turn her car towards his so that he could have some light to put the donut on.

Chanda began to walk back to her car, but she stopped, turned back around and said, "Sean, I think you should go home. We all know you are here to find out what happened to Karen that night. You are going to get yourself killed. Look what happened tonight. I think that this was a warning to you."

"Chanda, do you know something that I don't? Do you know who killed Karen?"

She turned quickly and walked back to her car. She turned her car towards Sean and watched him as he changed his tire...then without a word when he was done, she pulled off. Chanda couldn't dare tell Sean what she knew.

16

CHANDA POWERS PROM DAY
2003...

"Chanda, we need to talk about this now!"

"Mom, you are so annoying! Why would you be listening in on my phone conversation? I can't wait to graduate and get out of here; you are so controlling!"

"Chanda, do not speak to me like that! I want to know what will ruin your scholarship offer. You know that I can't afford to send you to that school. You worked hard all these years...I'm confused as to why you would lose it?

I know if my mother knew what I was caught up in, she would be so disappointed. It's been me and mom since my dead-beat father left to pursue his music career. He told my mom that if he stayed, he would only grow to resent us both, and that he had to follow his heart. We never heard from him again.

My whole life, my mom has pushed me to be the best at everything. She wanted more for me; she was a high-school dropout and married my father when she was 18. He was in control of everything, and when he left, he took everything with him. My mom had to work two jobs the whole time I was growing up. I remember being seven or eight and sitting in the backseat of my mom's car while she worked an 8-hour shift. She gave me milk in a small container and a peanut butter and jelly sandwich. She worked so hard. I can't let her down.

"Look, it's not a *what* it's a *who*, but don't worry about it. Montel's dad is going to take care of everything. I'm sorry that I yelled before. I am just really stressed, and I want tonight to be perfect."

Letting out a long breath, my mother replied, "Ok, I want the best for you, and the only way I see you having a bright future is by you getting out of here and going to college."

I walked over to my mom and gave her a kiss on the forehead, "I know mom, everything will be fine. I promise."

I was trying to hide the concern on my face, because the truth is that if Karen opens her big mouth, I can forget about my scholarship and possibly my freedom. Thinking about how she is trying to ruin my life enraged me. My phone buzzed...I took it out of my pocket and see that I have several missed calls from Courtney. I'm really not in the mood for her drama.

"Hey, Court!"

"I HATE her, she's going to pay!"

"Court, Court!! What is going on? Who are you talking about?"

"KAREN!" she yelled. "I took a bat to Jordan's car! My mom came home and grounded me, and now I can't go to the dance! And to make it worse, Jordan is still going. I can't believe her! She ruined what is supposed to be one of the most memorable nights of my life. There is no way I'm going to let her get away with this!"

"Courtney, you need to calm down! I have a plan..."

I went into detail with Courtney on how we would get even with Karen. I had to have a backup plan just in case Montel's father doesn't come through. I need Karen to keep her mouth shut, and there is only one way to ensure that she does that.

Sniffling, Courtney said, "You have been around me too long. I might not be going to prom, but after tonight, Karen will wish she never went."

17

Sean sat in his car trying to gather himself, but the longer he sat, the angrier he became. He could not believe that someone tried to run him off the road. He had received their message loud and clear; now it was his turn.

Sean knew it was a bad idea, but he didn't care. He called Tony and asked for the address of former Detective Montgomery. After a brief protest, Tony gave Sean the address.

"Tony, I need you to do one more favor for me. I don't know what is going to happen when I go over to Montgomery's house. Can you call the Cap and let her know that I may need to call in my favor tonight?" Before Tony could reply, Sean hung up.

Sean put the address in his phone's GPS. He jerked his wheel to the left, doing a U-turn, and drove down the street. All the memories and emotions of the night of Karen's murder began to take over Sean's mind, and he began to drive faster. Even though it had been a decade since his life was turned upside down, he still held a lot of resentment towards his city, but most of it was aimed at the man whose house he was headed to.

Shelia told Sean on multiple occasions that he should probably see a therapist, but Sean felt that a real man handled his feelings and emotions on his own. Besides, he didn't need anyone telling him how he should or shouldn't feel. The only thing that he needed was to solve the murder, and then he would be fine. He would have kept the promise he made to Karen as he held her lifeless body in his arms.

You have arrived at your location. 1919 Arrlington Drive. Sean hit the button to turn off the GPS. He slowly drove up the long driveway, finally approaching the huge brick house that was clearly paid for with Montgomery's salary from the Kingsley Corp. There was no way that a former detective could afford that home from his police pension. Sitting by the two-car garage was the familiar black Town Car with tinted windows. Sean ran up the wide fanned-out stairs and rang the doorbell. He waited, and no one came to the door, so he rang it again. He could hear a voice, but it was faint...then footsteps came closer and closer.

Sean's heart began to pound as the front door opened up. He was finally standing face to face with former Detective Landen Montgomery. He did not look as crispy as he did on the news. Gray and white stubble speckled his face from his chin to his ears. He had on a white t-shirt and checkered blue and maize pajama pants, which you could see hanging under his halfway zipped up, dark blue house coat.

He didn't look as big and intimidating as Sean remembered. Before Sean could say a word Landen Montgomery scoffed, "Do I know you? What are you doing at my door?"

Sean exclaimed, "You want to start with games? I see you haven't changed. I remember all the games you played when you tried to frame me for Karen's murder. The only difference now is that I have a badge, and you don't."

A smile spread across Montgomery's face, and he said, "Sean McKnight? Is that you, boy? I haven't seen you in years...but I see you still have the same bad attitude and smart mouth that got you in all that trouble to begin with."

Nostrils flaring, Sean replied, "Look, I am not here on a social call. Someone driving a car very similar to the one parked over there in your driveway tried to run me off the road tonight."

Folding his arms, Montgomery replied, "Son, are you accusing me? I have been in the house all night with my lovely wife, and I am 100% sure she will attest to that. Now, I suggest you get off my property before I get mad...and I can promise you, you don't want to see that."

Laughing, Sean said, "First of all, I am not your son." He stepped closer to Montgomery, looking him straight in the eye and said, "Secondly, I am not that scared little boy you intimidated and framed. I am a grown man, and I promise you, I am going to make you, and whoever put you up to framing me, pay. I know that you know who murdered Karen, and before I leave, I am going to watch handcuffs be tightened around your wrists. Do you remember what you told me that night? You said if it was the last thing you did, you were going to make sure I spent the rest of my life in jail. Now I am telling you...if it is the last thing that I do, I will make sure that you go from this lavish home to a cold 6 by 8 cell."

Without another word, Sean turned and walked away. Montgomery slammed his door, and Sean drove back out the long driveway.

Walking to his office, Landen picked up his phone, "We need to meet ASAP...we have a problem."

18

DETECTIVE LANDEN MONTGOMERY PROM DAY
2003...

"Look, Mr. Kingsley, there is not enough money in the world that would make me do that. She's a little girl. I am sure that there has to be another way of keeping her quiet. Have you tried talking to her parents? Maybe you can offer money to them for her silence?"

Craig Kingsley began to point his bony little finger in my face. If he didn't need it to sign my paychecks, I would break it.

Craig said, "You will do as you are told. Since when did you develop morals? May I remind you that I am personal friends with the district attorney, mayor, and governor. Let's not forget to mention the millions my family has donated to the Fraternal Order of Police. It would be a shame if it was leaked out that there is a dirty detective on the force. I am sure you wouldn't want to lose that police pension that I hear about."

I despise him! Everything he has, he was given. Unlike me, I have had to work all my life for everything. I didn't have a rich daddy ready to sign over the family business to me. Craig's father, Mathis Kingsley, was a real man. He moved here from the south and built this company from nothing. If he was in this situation, he would handle things himself. He would use his power and influence to cause so much trouble for the girl and her family that she would keep her mouth shut. The only reason I still work for the family is at Mathis Kingsley's request. When he moved to Florida, he knew that his son would need all the help he could get.

I threw my hands in the air and said, "The threats are not necessary. I'll do it, but this is going to cost you. You have to put it in writing that you will hire me to work for your corporation when I retire from the police force...I want to be head of security. I want to make six figures. Let's be clear, don't ever threaten me again. If I go down, I'll take your whole company down with me."

They think I'm some dumb cop, but when I started doing odd jobs for the Kingsley family decades ago, I started taping conversations and making copies of documents that I could use as insurance just in case they ever tried to double cross me. I know how these rich types work, I won't be their sacrificial lamb.

I put on my sunglasses and began to walk back to my car when my phone rang.

————

"What can I do for you, Williams?"

Williams replied "Montgomery, we have a bad one. Meet me at Willow Run High School...there has been a murder."

I grabbed my light, put it on top of my cruiser and turned on my sirens. I quickly maneuvered around the spiral driveway out into the street. When I arrived on the scene, there were over a dozen patrol cars there with lights flashing. I took out my badge and flipped it so that my shield was visible, and one of the patrol men lifted the yellow "Do Not Cross" scene tape for me to go under.

"What do we have?"

Williams replied, "The victim is 17-year-old Karen LaSalle."

I felt a cold chill go down my back. This is the very girl that Craig

Kingsley had just talked to me about. The girl that was going to expose his son Montel and a couple of his friends.

"Are you there, Montgomery?"

"Yeah, yeah...it's such a shame. I have a young niece her age. I don't know what I would do if something like this happened to her... ok, any witnesses or suspects?"

Williams exclaimed, "No one actually saw the murder, but witnesses said when they came out, her boyfriend, Sean McKnight, was holding her in his arms. The boy has blood all over him. We have not been able to locate the murder weapon."

"McKnight huh...well that boy is trouble. I know his family; he comes from a bad bloodline. Have you questioned him at all yet?"

"No, I have him sitting in a patrol car. The crowd began to get rowdy, and I didn't want them to hurt him. To be honest, the kid looked genuinely sad."

"Don't let that boy fool you...save your sympathy for the VIC and her family."

"Victim, Montgomery, victim." Williams asserted.

Detective Treat Williams has been on the force for 15 years. He had been a detective for 3 years now. I trained him when he first came to our precinct. The first year, he never dared to question me. At times, I may have gone against regulations. After the second year working together, he would sometimes question my methods. He hated to hear victims be referred to as "the VIC". It was a cold and callous term to him.

I told him that he would also one day start calling the victims that. It comes with the job people become VICS, the family of the VIC, and suspects. After you've been doing this for as long as I have, you learn to remove the emotions. It's the only way to deal with some of the inhumane things that we encounter.

Detective Williams was adamant with me that he would never refer to a victim that way. He told me that his mother was murdered at their family's gas station when he was 10 years old. He remembered hearing one of the officers refer to him as "the VIC's son." He didn't know what it meant at the time, but he remembered how it made him feel, and when he became an officer, he swore that he would never use that term. He said if the day came when he did, he would put in his papers.

———

After examining the body and talking to a few witnesses, I darted towards the patrol car and yanked that punk out by his collar. I yelled to the patrolman to walk away, and then I slammed Sean against the cruiser.

Detective Williams was right behind me and protested, "Detective Montgomery! Stop! We will question him at the station, but not like this. Besides, we need to get him out of that shirt and jacket...we don't want the evidence tainted."

Unclenching my jaws, I whispered to Sean, "If it's the last thing I do, I am going to make sure you spend the rest of your rotten life in jail." I let go of Sean, pushing him back into the patrol car. I went to the officer and ordered him to get Sean to the station.

19

"I can't imagine why this could not wait until the morning; everything is always so urgent with you!" Craig Kingsley said in contempt.

Montgomery replied, "We have trouble. Sean McKnight...Detective Sean McKnight. He confirmed that he is here to find out who murdered that girl ten years ago, the night of prom. He also knows that I tried to run him off the road tonight, and I am a direct connection to you and your company. It's only a matter of time before he puts it all together."

Craig exclaimed, "Until he puts what together?"

"You know, the murder. You and Mathis were very clear that you wanted me to frame Sean for her murder. Why would you want that unless you or someone in your family had something to do with it? Like Montel?"

Large veins began to poke out of the side of Craig's head. Walking towards Landen Montgomery, he replied, "You keep my son's name out of your mouth. As I recall, you were oh so ready to frame the boy. It didn't take much convincing. We had nothing to do with it. We wanted her scared and silent, not dead."

Landen had been in love with Sean's mother since they were in high school, but she was not attracted to him. She only had eyes for the 6'3", broad shouldered rebel, who was a high school dropout and 5 years older than both Landen and her. No one saw the side of him that Sean's mother did. She loved that he was a big dreamer, and he wasn't afraid to take chances. Even though her mother forbade her to date him, she did anyway. A year after she graduated, she became pregnant, and her boyfriend went to jail for bashing a man's head in during a bar fight.

While she was pregnant, Landen still tried to date her, and she turned him down repeatedly, telling him she was only focused on making the best life for her son. Landen hated the unborn child...he blamed the baby for keeping him away from the love of his life. Landen's love for Sean's mother quickly turned to spite and hate. He went to the police academy, and afterwards, he was hired into the Ypsilanti Police Department. He would often harass Sean and his friends when they were teenagers, and when he did, he always made it a point to tell Sean to say hello to his mother.

"Yeah, well I had my own reasons for framing him, but if he starts poking his nose around, he might find out about what you've been doing...and then what?" Montgomery exclaimed.

Pointing his finger, he replied, "You worry about Sean and let me worry about my business. We pay you really good money...NOW, DO YOUR JOB!"

Taking a deep breath, trying to convince himself of why it would be a horrible idea to choke this man, Montgomery replied, "I have friends on the force. I'll see if I can have them run him out of town. By the way, yesterday, he stopped by that Ms. Mary's house. She is still refusing to sell Kingsley Corp her property. Once she sells, I'm sure the others who are holding out will follow suit."

Tapping his fingers on his desk, Craig said, "I thought you said she was sick and didn't have much longer."

"That's what I was told. The stubborn old lady is fighting it."

Sighing, Craig replied, "I need you to take care of her. Every day she does not sign is costing my company money. I already lost one investor, and the others are becoming very nervous. Do whatever you need to. I don't want father feeling like I can't run the business."

Walking towards the door, Montgomery said, "I look forward to my bonus check at the end of the year."

He walked down the long hallway leading to the large, arched-shaped front door with beautiful stained-glass windows surrounding it.

He sat in his car flipping through the radio stations until he landed on the sports channel. He picked up his phone and texted: *Call me ASAP. I have a job for you.*

20

The phones were ringing non-stop; this always happened when there's a full moon. Some say it's superstition, but there is something about it that affects criminals, the mentally ill, and pregnant women. That is why all hands are on deck, and Detective Treat Williams and his partner, Detective Fields, are working.

They had already received one call from a lady who barely made it to her front porch when the baby decided it was time to come out. They had three disorderly conduct calls, two sightings of UFO's, one call about a fight at the bowling alley, (both parties were long gone before the police made it), and a phone call about a car trying to run another car off the road. When the police came to the scene the cars were gone but skid marks were there, and a blown-out tire was on the gravel.

Detective Williams had had about enough, when he received a call about a man on the sidewalk trying to sell air in mason jars. After reassuring the concerned citizen that he would send a patrol car out as soon as possible, he told Detective Fields that he was stepping out for fresh air. Detective Williams grabbed his Ypsilanti Police Department Jacket which was a permanent fixture on the back of his chair. It was 70 degrees that morning, but the temperature had dropped 30 degrees, and it was chilly...of course this was not surprising weather for Michigan.

The phones had stopped ringing, so Detective Fields used this opportunity to call his wife to see how her day was going and to check on their son. Grayson was 5 years old and had been diagnosed with cancer, but he was fighting, like the champ that he is. His wife could no longer work; she had to become the primary caregiver. Detective Fields tried to work as much overtime as he could to cover all the medical bills.

However, even after the station held a fundraiser for his family and receiving a donation from a non-profit that helps police officers with medical bills, they still owed money for Grayson's treatments. He was receiving an experimental treatment that their insurance company refused to cover, and they were very expensive...but the treatments seemed to be working, and Detective Fields would do anything to give his son more time.

After getting off the phone with his wife, Detective Fields felt a buzz in his pocket. He had a message from former Detective Montgomery. It said: *call me ASAP. I have a job for you.* His heart began to race. He wished he had never said 'Yes', the first time that Landen Montgomery asked him to intimidate someone into selling their home to Kingsley Corp, but he was offered $5,000.00, and he needed that for the first payment for his son's treatments.

After the first request, he was asked to do jobs more frequently, but Detective Fields decided he was no longer going to take any more jobs, after Landen Montgomery asked him to get information on a fellow officer. He did it, but he felt horrible. He hoped nothing happened to the young detective, whose name was Sean McKnight.

Rubbing his brow, he texted back: *I'll call in a few when my partner comes back...he went out to get fresh air leaving me to man the phones.*

About 30 minutes later, Detective Williams walked back into the station with a smile on his face and two cups of coffee. He sat one down in front of Detective Fields, then went to his chair and sat down. He looked up, and Detective Fields' face was pale.

"Fields, is everything ok. Is your son ok?"

Rubbing his hands together, Detective Fields rose to his feet and said, "Yes, everything is fine. I think I'm going to step out for a bit."

"I would grab a jacket if I were you," warned Detective Williams

He replied, "I'm okay, the cold air will do me some good."

Detective Williams shrugged his shoulders as Fields headed towards the door.

———————

Fields pulled the collar of his shirt up in an attempt to cover his ears and began rubbing his hands in a circular motion, hoping to cause some friction that would warm them. He wished he had listened to Williams and grabbed a jacket. He looked up at the sky and could only see a few stars; not like back at home in Colorado. He thought about when he was young lying out in his parent's back yard trying to count the stars, but they were endless. Life was so simple then.

His family owned a ranch, and on it they had horses. Fields and his dad would go out for long rides, and they always ended up at their pond fishing. He wished he could do those types of things with his son, but the treatments leave him too weak to do much. The ranch was passed down from Fields' grandfather to his father...and Fields' father taught him from a young age how to run a ranch, hoping to one day pass it down to him.

Fields' father was disappointed when he told him that he was not interested in the family's ranch, and that he planned to go to the Marines, and then join the police force. They didn't talk much after that.

Fields walked away from the building for privacy. Approaching him was an officer who had handcuffs on a familiar face. Her name was Trish. She was 6 feet tall and had on black pleather shorts and fishnet stockings, which had a hole on the left side, near her thigh.

Her high boots almost reached the hole, but they weren't quite high enough. Her red shirt barely made it to her belly button. Tonight, she was wearing a red wig. As the officer was escorting her into the station, he could hear her trying to explain why she stabbed her "John."

Fields pulled out his phone to call Mongomery. "Hi, look, I've been thinking about it, and I don't want to do any more jobs for money. When you asked me to get personal information on a fellow officer that crossed the line."

Yelling, Landen replied, "You will quit when I say you quit. I own you. I have enough information on you to make you lose your job, insurance, and pension. Where does that leave your son? Look, this will be the last time, and we will make sure you don't have to worry about money again. I need you to make a visit to Ms. Mary Hall, and when you leave, I need you to make sure she signs over her house. I'm sure she has plenty of blue envelopes lying around. Find one with the lowest offer and make her sign it."

Looking around, Fields whispered, "But what if she doesn't sign it?"

"Then you sign it for her. Look up, across the street."

Fields looked up and saw a black Town Car with tinted windows; there was a hand flagging him towards the car. He slowly walked closer; it was Landen Montgomery...he handed Fields a black, leather pouch. Fields opened it, and it was full of money. Montgomery told him that after the job was done, there was much more money where that came from.

Smiling, Montgomery said, "Oh, yeah, to answer your question... if she won't sign the paper, in the pouch, on the bottom, there is a syringe...it's better if you don't know what's in it. Put it into her IV so no marks are left on the body." He pulled off, with a smirk on his face.

Fields stood there in disbelief...*did he just ask me to kill someone?* A horn blew and made Fields jump; he realized that he was standing in the middle of the road. He darted back across the street to his car. He opened his trunk and took another look at the cash in the pouch. He pulled out his wallet and stared at the family portrait, that he would so proudly pull out when asked about his family. A tear rolled down his cheek and landed on the photo. He wiped his face, sat the pouch down, closed the trunk and then headed back inside the station. He knew what he had to do for his family.

21

Sean could not get the encounter with Landen Montgomery out of his mind. He was agitated and could not believe the audacity of that man. He pulled into his grandmothers' driveway, laid the seat back and took a deep breath. He had been dreading going back to her home and going through her things, but tonight was as good of a night as any. Sean felt he needed to step away from the case at least until the morning. His head was not clear, and that could cause him to miss something crucial.

The neighbors had started complaining about the grass and weeds that were taking over his grandmother's yard, so Sean hired a company to come out twice a month to keep the grass cut and pull the weeds; and in the winter, they would come out and plow.

He knew that he could not keep the house. Shelia and Sean discussed the pros and cons. She wanted to get rid of it right away, but Sean wasn't ready. Now, since they have another child on the way, the family could use the money. Sean gripped the steering wheel until the palm of his hand turned white. The thought of selling the house brought him great anxiety. Even though he had a pretty rough childhood, the house was a happy reminder of the good times, and he knew as a child that he was always safe and had stability at his grandmothers.

As early as he could remember, his mom would pull up into the driveway and say *You be a good boy for your grandma. I'll be back in a few days.* As the years went by, the few days would become a few weeks, a few months, and eventually a few years. He knew his mother loved him; he never blamed her. His grandmother would say *Ya momma is sick, boy, If she could keep you with her all the time, she would. It's because she loves you, that she brings you here to a safe place while she gets well.*

His eyes became watery, and a lump began growing bigger and bigger in his throat. Sean sat up and opened the car door to get some fresh air. He had a "Beware of Dog" sign put into the window, hoping it would deter thieves and vandals, although the neighbors knew that the house was vacant. Tony told Sean about a device that serves as both a doorbell and a video surveillance camera, and that his phone would alert him if anyone was in his yard. He never purchased it for his grandmother's house, but he was definitely going to install one at his own home.

Sean opened the screen door, and it made a squeaky sound. He made a mental note to go to the garage and grab a can of DW-40 on his way out and spray the hinges. He unlocked the door and slowly turned the knob. Then, he reached over and pulled the cord on his grandmother's favorite lamp; it was green and had big fake crystals dangling from the shade. It wasn't his style, but he loved it because his grandmother loved it. He was going to have it shipped to Rhode Island with some other things he wanted to keep. He decided that the rest of the items were going to be donated to different local charities. He knew that was what his grandmother would have wanted; she was such a generous person. The one thing about his grandmother, she always kept a tidy home and took care of the things that she owned.

Sean walked down the hallway to his grandmother's room. He remembered, as a child, he would often have nightmares and his grandmother would come get him and put him in her bed. She would warm him milk, and sometimes, if she had baked earlier in the day, she would bring him cookies or a piece of her famous zucchini bread.

The day after Karen died and Sean was released from police custody into his grandmother care. He lay in that bed with her for hours crying and pleading with her to believe that he would never do anything to hurt Karen.

Sean opened the door to her room. The bed that was a safe haven for him, looked so much smaller. He wished his grandmother was there; he would curl up by her, knowing that she would say the right things. She would give him the comfort that he needed at that very moment. He picked up a picture of both of them, that was right next to the bed, and held it close to his heart as he whispered, *I love you Grandma,* as tears streamed down his face.

Knowing that his time was limited, he decided to go through some of her papers and shred them. He opened the closet where she kept a black, five-drawer filing cabinet. He pulled the top drawer, but it would not budge...it was locked. He knew where his grandmother kept the key; he had peeked one time when she told him to turn around and close his eyes.

Sean walked over to the picture of his grandparents on their wedding day, his grandmother in a beautiful lace dress, and his grandfather in his army uniform. They looked so happy. Rumor had it that the war is what turned his grandfather into an alcoholic, which later caused him to take his own life. Sean looked at the picture. He didn't seem to resemble either of his grandparents, and his mother didn't either. Sean took the brown cardboard covering on the back of the picture frame off, and there was a small, gold key. He went back to the closet, stuck the key in the lock and opened the top drawer. There were files neatly placed in it and labeled by month and year. It was decades of paperwork...this was going to be a bigger task than he had time for.

He started pillaging through the files and noticed a box all the way in the back. He grabbed it, walked over to the bed and sat down. It was full of cards, letters, and pictures. He pulled out a stack of letters that had a red bow tied around them.

Sean carefully opened the brittle, yellow stained letter it read:

August 4, 1965

My Dearest Mattie,

Every moment away from you is like an eternity. How I wish that you could be mine. I look forward to the next time that I see you. I often wonder what life for us would have been like if I met you a few years earlier. Your love for me would have never let you marry that man.

You are the only one who knows the real me. You know who I am behind the tough exterior. You bring out the loving, caring person in me. Just know that your smile brightens my world. If I could - I would get rid of the man who is keeping us apart. I know that you don't like when I talk like that, but you even said that he is not the man you married.

I hope the money enclosed with this letter helps take care of some of your bills. I wish you would leave that drunk. He cannot even provide for you, and don't blame the war for his behavior. I don't know why you always take up for him like that; with the way he treats you. I know that we could never marry, but the thought of you with him drives me crazy.

I love you my dear, and I can't wait until the next time I see you.

XOXO,

MAK

Sean could not believe what he was reading. *Who was this man? Did his grandmother have some sort of relationship with him?* He lay back on his grandmothers' floral comforter. If she was there, she would have said, *"Boy, get your tail off my bed with your outside clothes on."*

Every letter in the stack was from this MAK. He knew that if anyone knew who this person was, it would be Ms. Mary. Sean closed the filing cabinet and locked it. With the key in his hand, he went back over to the tall, brown, wooden dresser and picked up the picture of his grandparents. He stared at it for a moment, not sure he knew the woman in that picture at all. He turned the picture over and placed the key back where he had taken it from.

22

S ean lay in the bed at the hotel wide awake. He was so confused. Was his grandmother having an affair or was this just someone who was in love with her? He looked at the pile of letters next to him, afraid to read any more, in fear that he might find the answer to his questions.

Reaching across the bed, he shoved the stack of letters onto the floor. He watched the red numbers on the clock, as they went from 3:00am to 6:00am. There was no need for him to go to sleep; all he wanted to do was to go see Ms. Mary. He hoped she could give him any answers, and he just wanted to check on her; he knew that she would not be around too much longer.

Sean turned his head and got a quick whiff from his armpit. He couldn't go back to sleep, but he definitely needed a shower before heading out. He began regretting even coming to Michigan; he was no closer to finding Karen's murderer. He had more questions than answers.

With a white towel secured around his waist, Sean walked over to the desk where he had a couple of pictures from Karen's crime scene. He had looked at them a thousand times. They were etched in his mind. He always wondered why Karen was near the opposite side of the parking lot from where they had parked. She would have run towards their car, but maybe she was so upset, she forgot where they parked.

Once again, more questions than answers. Sean slid into his jeans and put on his green polo shirt. He still had time to get downstairs for the continental breakfast; it was available from 6am-10am. After 10am, there were only bagels and coffee.

———

Sean sat at the back table in the lobby eating his omelet and finishing off his last piece of wheat toast, that had grape jelly neatly spread over it. He could not get those darn letters out of his head, and against his better judgment, he opened another one. This one was much shorter, and the tone was a lot less loving.

July 1966

Mattie,

This can never get out. I'm a very important person in this city. Are you sure, Mattie? How do I know that you are not just trying to get more money from me. I tell you about how quickly things are happening for my business, and then you tell me you are pregnant. How do I know that the baby is mine?

My wife and I just had a boy. This will ruin me. I'll continue to support you, but I don't ever want to see you, and don't you ever bring that baby around here. The money will come monthly, but this is the last letter.

MAK

Sean's grandfather always suspected that the child wasn't his; he would always say she was too light to be his, and that his whole family has hazel eyes...all his brothers' kids had hazel eyes. He never had much of a relationship with Sean's mother. Besides, he took his life when she was a toddler.

Sean drank the last bit of his coffee and headed towards the door. He had to talk to Ms. Mary now.

23

Detective Fields could not believe he allowed things to go this far. He sat in his car and watched as Ms. Mary's nurse walked out. He dipped down in his seat so that she could not see him. The neighbor's kitchen light was on, so he decided to enter from the back.

He was sweating profusely as he pried open the window, just enough that he could squeeze in. He stood over Ms. Mary as she slept peacefully in her bed. He went to look for one of the letters that he needed to have her sign. He was going to put a pen in her hand and guide her signature as she slept.

His phone rang, and he pushed the side button to ignore the call; he could not be distracted. The phone rang again; when he looked down, it was his wife.

"Honey, is everything ok?"

"No, I had to call the ambulance to take Grayson to the hospital. He's not breathing!! EMS is working on him now. I can't lose him. I'm not ready to say goodbye to our son."

Fields replied, "He is going to be fine. I know it. He is a strong boy. You think positive, you hear me?"

Gasping, she said, "He's breathing! Hurry and meet us at the hospital!! I already called the oncologist's office, and they said they would page the doctor on call to meet us at the hospital."

Whispering, Fields said, "I'm about to leave work, and I will meet you guys there. I love you honey; trust me, everything is going to be ok."

"We are in the ambulance now...please hurry!!"

Fields went back through Ms. Mary's room. He felt the syringe in his pocket. He went out the window, regretting ever going in there. How could he even consider taking another life, after all that he was doing to save his son's.

He ran back to the car and called Landen Montgomery as he drove away to the hospital.

24

Sean barely stopped his car, before he jumped out and began to run over to Mr. Mary's yard. There was an ambulance and a sea of lights flashing from police cars. A tall, young officer with bright red, curly hair and a nose covered in freckles stood at the front gate, carefully guarding who entered the scene.

Sean felt around for his badge, hoping that if he flashed it quickly, the young officer wouldn't realize that he wasn't supposed to be there. Sean put his charming smile on his face and said, "Hello, they are expecting me." He flashed his badge, the officer did a quick glance and moved out of the way for Sean. From experience, he knew that most young officers would not question their superior.

Sean entered the house, and a stern voice said, "Hey, how did he get in here?" Pointing directly at Sean.

With his hands in the air, Sean said, "I'm about to reach in my pocket for my badge...please don't shoot. I am Detective Sean McKnight from Rhode Island, and Ms. Mary is a friend."

Detective Fields said, "I don't care who you are, you have no authority to be here."

"Sean...Detective McKnight. It has been a long time!" Coming from a voice across the room.

The short, muscular officer stepped from behind Fields and said, "It's fine, he can stay...maybe he can answer some questions for us."

Sean immediately recognized the voice as Detective Williams. He looked a lot different; he had definitely been to the gym regularly. The last time Sean encountered him, he was small in stature, now he looked like he could compete in a bodybuilding contest. When Sean was arrested for Karen's murder, he was the only one who treated him fairly and decently. He quickly realized that that was the voice of the person who called him and left the box at the front desk of the hotel. Landen Montgomery's ex-partner. No wonder there is so much in that box that was not in the official evidence.

Sean nodded at Detective Williams, both keeping the secret quietly between them. Then Sean said, "Do you know what happened? I just visited her. I knew she was sick, but ..."

Sean began to think, *Why are detectives here, if this death was by natural cause?* He asked, "Why are you here? Do you suspect foul play?"

Detective Fields replied, "We received a call from Ms. Mary's nurse; she found her this morning when she came in to change her IV bag. She said that she was sitting in the living room, which was odd at that time of the morning. A neighbor came by and told the nurse he saw someone leaving out of her house around 3am. The nurse left at 11pm and locked up."

Hoping that neither of the seasoned detectives noticed the nervousness in his voice, Fields said, "McKnight, where were you at 3am?"

Sean said abruptly, "In the bed at the hotel staring at the walls. I'm sure the hotel has video of me entering and then leaving this morning to come visit Ms. Mary."

Detective Williams chimed in, "Detective McKnight, so what brought you over here this morning?"

"I'm leaving tomorrow, so I wanted to make sure that I was able to see Ms. Mary again before I left."

He was not going to tell them he was there because he needed to know who his real grandfather was. Sean lowered his head from the shame of it all.

Lifting his head, Sean said, "Can I go over to her body?"

Fields was about to object, when Williams blurted out, "That's fine...wait for me to escort you over. Until we confirm your alibi, you are technically still a person of interest. This is going against every guideline written, but I think that I'll give you some leeway, considering all our department put you through...this is the least I could do."

Fields did not want McKnight near the body; his presence made him very nervous. What if McKnight carefully examined Ms. Mary and found something. Fields was working hard to convince everyone on the scene that Ms. Mary had a heart attack or some other complication from her illness.

Sean bent down next to Ms. Mary. He bowed his head, saying a quick prayer. He stood back up wiping the tears that began to fill his eyes. Sean felt a little guilty because he was thinking she was his only hope of finding who MAK was.

Detective McKnight pointed down to something on Ms. Mary's night gown. Williams yelled for the crime scene investigators to come over; he showed them the small hairs that were on Ms. Mary's nightgown.

Ms. Mary wore a wig; Sean remembered being a young boy and finding them in her closet. He was amazed by the different colors and length of the wigs that she had. She had alopecia, which she developed in her 30s, and eventually, she had no hair on her body. She gave up the other wigs and only wore a curly, gray wig. The hair that Sean found could've been nothing, but in a possible murder investigation, you look over all the evidence.

The petite, young, crime scene investigator grabbed her tweezers and slowly picked the hairs one by one and put them into the small plastic baggy…after grabbing the last one, she looked at Sean and said, "Good eye, I'll get these pieces of hair and the other evidence over to the lab as soon as possible."

Sean forced a smile. His heart hurt too badly at the moment for conversation. He turned around and said to Detective Williams, "Please keep me updated with whatever information that you can share."

25

Sean rolled his windows down to let the cool, morning air hit his face. He kept thinking about Ms. Mary from when he first came into town; she was moving around, laughing, and she would not stop talking. He was no doctor, but he just could not believe that she had had a heart attack.

A smile came across his face as he thought about the last time Ms. Mary, his grandma, and mother were all together. He was about 9 years old, and his mother had just gotten back from one of her many trips to rehab. The court gave her a choice between 6 months in jail or going into an inpatient facility for 3 months.

He watched as the three most important woman in his life laughed, played cards, and ate. His mother had the most beautiful smile he had ever seen. She used to smile all the time before the drugs and drinking. Sean sat as close as he could to her; she kissed him on the forehead and showed him her hand. Even though he was not allowed to play cards with the adults, he and his mom played all the time together at home. Sean looked up at her with bright eyes, knowing that the joker, ace of spades, king of spades, and jack of spades that she had left in her hand was a sure win for her.

As she slammed down her last card, she jumped up and did her victory dance. This was followed by a debate about whether the cards were shuffled good enough, and Ms. Mary grabbing the cards, saying she was going to go pull out a different deck. Everyone in the room burst out laughing.

Shelia often asked Sean why he didn't like playing cards. He would tell her it's not fun to him. The truth is, that it brought up too many memories, and along with those memories, unbearable pain.

Sean is now back up in his room. Sitting down on the chair by the desk, he opens the box of evidence again, hoping that he will find something in there that he missed. He knew it was a long shot, but he was hoping for a Hail Mary; he only had 10 hours before the last event for their reunion, and he was no closer to solving the murder than when he first came home.

He pulled out everything...he put the pictures in a pile, the witness statements, Montgomery's and Williams' notes, and all the evidence that was gathered at the scene. He pulled out the picture with the close up of Karen's face; there was a mark on her face...four tiny squares, with a small circle.

The detectives were sure that the bruising was caused some time during her murder. They compared pictures taken of Karen before and during the dance, and there were no signs of any facial injury.

The medical examiner's report said, "It appeared the suspect struck the victim with their hand and left a contusion, along with an unidentified impression." The medical examiner suggested that it may have been from a ring.

Sean looked down at his watch with the big, silver face surrounded by diamonds, with its black leather strap. It was a 5-year anniversary gift from Shelia, and on the back of the watch, she had engraved, "Love you forever. Shelia."

It was 4:30pm. Sean had gotten lost in the evidence and didn't even realize how late it was. He picked up the phone to shoot Shelia a quick text. He decided not to call her because she would have detected the sadness and frustration in his voice, and he did not want to worry her.

His phone started buzzing in his hand; it was from the Ypsilanti Police Department.

"Hello, this is Detective McKnight."

"Hey, Detective, this is Detective Williams. We have had some interesting developments regarding Ms. Mary's case over the past few hours. After you found the small hairs on her, I decided we needed to do a more thorough look. I had CSI to go back and examine her body and home more thoroughly. The pretty young investigator, who I think has a crush on you, found a partial thumbprint on the IV bag. I'm having the hair and thumbprint rushed to our forensics analyst. I'll keep you updated."

Sean sighed and said, "Thank you, Detective, for the update. Thank you for all the help you have given me. It doesn't look like I'm going to find the answers I've been looking for, but hopefully we can find answers for Ms. Mary."

Who would try to kill Ms. Mary? She was terminal. Sean thought about all the blue envelopes that he saw on her table and her couch. He couldn't remember seeing them when he was there earlier, but he also was not thinking about mail. He could not shake the feeling that the two were connected in some way. He would not put anything past the Kingsleys Ms. Mary was clearly stopping their plans; maybe they didn't want to wait for her to sign over her property any longer.

He went to the closet and pulled out his blue, tailored suit, black dress shirt, his blue, black, and grey flowered tie, and a pocket square. He laid the clothes neatly across the bed. Then he went into his suitcase and grabbed his nicely polished black loafers. The weekend had not gone the way he wanted. He thought that he would find the few missing pieces that he needed to solve Karen's murder by now. He began to contemplate not even going to the last night of the reunion and taking a flight home and surprising Shelia. But there was something deep down that told him to just go.

26

Fields rushed back up to the hospital as soon as they left the crime scene. He wanted to take the opportunity to see his son before anything urgent at work popped up. He entered the pediatric wing of the hospital and walked past the Big Bird statue on the way to the clerk's desk. He was amused, thinking about the first time Grayson came to the hospital and saw the statue; he turned around and ran back to his mother, grabbing her leg, and insisting she picked him up and walk as far away from Big Bird as possible.

Fields' wife told him they were changing Grayson's room, but when he called back to find out what the room number was, her phone kept going to voicemail. He made his way to the information desk. Sitting there, was a familiar face. She was an older lady, who always wore a yellow dress and pearl earrings and necklace. She always greeted Fields and his family with a big smile. She told Fields that she started volunteering at the children's hospital when she lost her son after a long battle with cancer.

"Hello, Detective, I saw your wife earlier. I'm sorry to hear that Grayson is back in the hospital."

Fields replied, "Thank you! Would you mind looking up his room number for me? I can't get a hold of my wife."

"Of course," she started to tap on the keyboard and said, "Here we go...he is in room 1230."

"Thank you," Fields said, as he moved quickly towards the elevator.

He impatiently held the door for a group of nurses in blue scrubs, holding coffee cups in their hands. As the last one walked in, he hit the 'Close Elevator' button. The elevator was filled with the aroma of vanilla and pumpkin spice.

Fields walked down the hall looking at the room numbers. He finally made it to his son's room, which was at the end of the hall. He slowly opened the door, and there was his wife, asleep with her head lying next to their son on the bed. Fields walked quietly towards his son and gave him a kiss on his forehead.

His wife's head shot up. She said, "Baby, you scared me."

"I'm sorry, Honey," he whispered.

He walked around the bed, gave her a hug and said, "How is little man doing?"

"The doctors think it was a side effect from his treatments. They want to observe him another day, and then they will most likely discharge him."

"That's good news!" he said with a smile.

They both sat quietly watching their son as he slept. Both were grateful that he was still there with them.

Whispering, his wife said, "Babe, you seem a million miles away."

"I just caught a case today, and it's heavy on my mind. The truth is, we don't know if it's a homicide, or if they died by natural causes. I was there all morning and skipped coffee, that's all."

He would not dare tell his wife what he had been up to. She thought that the money for Grayson's treatments was coming from all the overtime he had been putting in at work, and he also told her that he had cashed in a couple of investments.

Even though everything that he had done was to get money for their son, he knew she would not approve.

27

Detective Williams was sitting at his desk, with his feet up on the table, twirling a pen around his fingers. He took a sip of his coffee and then leaned back in his chair. Everything inside of him told him that this was a murder. He did not believe Ms. Mary died of a heart attack.

He thought about the interview he had with Ms. Mary's beautiful, dark brown nurse, who had braids down to her waist, with neatly placed shells dangling from the sides. She had a small accent; maybe her family was from the islands. She said that Ms. Mary was in pain, she gave her a bath, changed her into her pajamas, and gave her pain meds that would have knocked her out for the night, so she does not know how Ms. Mary would have made it to her chair alone.

The nurse had to take a seat on the porch while talking to Detective Williams. She had just started working for hospice, and Ms. Mary was the first patient she had ever found dead. Before hospice, she worked as a labor and delivery nurse.

The phone rang, and Fields answered, "Detective Fields."

"Detective Fields, you and Detective Williams may want to come to my lab quickly. The ID on the thumbprint came back, and you won't believe whose it is."

Fields replied, "On our way." He looked up and said, "Williams, let's go!! We have to get over to Nina's lab...she has an ID on the thumbprint."

Scoffing, he replied, "Why didn't she just give you the name over the phone?"

Fields shrugged his shoulder and walked towards the door, and Williams swung his legs off the desk and hurried behind him.

It was very busy down in the lab. The night before had been chaotic, and they had tons of evidence they were working on, but evidence from a possible murder shot to the top of the list and became first priority.

Walking over to Detective Williams and Fields in her white lab coat, the tech said, "I wanted to give you this news in person. I wouldn't want this getting out before you have a chance to investigate." She looks around the room to ensure no one was listening and said, "The thumbprint belongs to former Detective Landen Montgomery."

Fields' face turned white as snow. He was relieved that it was not his thumbprint.

"Fields, are you there?"

Looking startled, Fields replied, "Oh, I'm sorry, my mind wandered for a moment."

Exhaling, Williams said, "I was saying...I don't want to cause any undue embarrassment for Montgomery; he was my partner for years. I learned everything from him. Let's go to his house and question him...I'm sure there is a reasonable explanation for this."

Wiping his brow with his hand, Fields agreed, and they headed to Montgomery's house. Fields was quiet the whole way there. He started to regret ever doing any of those jobs for Montgomery. Even though he made money for his son's healthcare, it wasn't right. Fields began to hit the passenger side door, and Williams pulled over. Before Williams could say a word, Fields was on the side of the road bent over, throwing up. He lifted his head up, leaned back against the car and looked up into the sky.

Williams rolled down the window and said, "Fields, do you need to go home? Are you ok?"

Fields opened the door, climbed in, and put his seat belt on. He assured Williams that he was fine to go with him. He just had had a long couple of days. Williams looked back over at Fields, pulled the gear down and drove off. 20 minutes later, they were pulling up into Landen Montgomery's driveway.

Montgomery was sitting on the porch drinking a beer. He stood up with a smile and said, "What an honor! Ypsi's finest paying me a visit. Would you fellas like a beer?"

Williams extended his hand to shake Montgomery's and said, "No, thank you, this is not a social call. I have a couple of questions I need to ask you."

Fields put his foot up on the porch but would not make eye contact with Montgomery in fear that Williams would feel the tension between them.

"Ok, don't just stand there, ask me the questions?"

Williams replied, "We are investigating the death of Ms. Mary."

"I heard about it. That's so sad."

Fields' head jerked up as he looked at Montgomery. Montgomery looked back at Fields with a sly smile forming across his face.

"What's so amusing?" Detective Williams protested.

"Oh, nothing, the young detective here reminds me of you, when you first came on the job. Quiet, observant, probably even obedient. The only difference is, I couldn't get you to keep your mouth shut."

Fields replied, "How well do you know Ms. Mary?"

Pointing his finger at Fields, Montgomery chuckled, "I guess he does talk...look, get to why you are here. You know that I know Ms. Mary. Anybody who has lived in this town for some time knows Ms. Mary."

Interrupting, Williams said, "When was the last time that you saw her?"

Rubbing his salt and pepper beard, Montgomery replied, "As a matter of fact, I went to see her yesterday. I'm sure you already know that, and that's why you are here."

"Landen, we didn't know you were there yesterday. Approximately what time would that have been, and do you visit her often?"

"It was before noon, and no, I don't visit often, but my wife ran into some of her friends from the neighborhood at the grocery store, and they told her that Ms. Mary didn't have much time to live, so I decided that I would go visit her. You know, she helped make our jobs easy. She kept everyone in that neighborhood in check. No one wanted to answer to Ms. Mary."

"Thank you, Landen. I knew that there must have been a reason your fingerprint was found at her house," said Williams.

Montgomery felt like his eyes were going to pop out of his head. He was sure that he wiped down everything in the house that he touched. He reached down, took a big gulp of beer and said, "If you detectives are done questioning me, I have some other business to attend to."

"Thank you for your time, Landen." Williams said.

As Williams and Fields were walking off the porch, both of their phones buzzed. They looked down at their texts, and then looked at each other. The text read: *The hairs found on the victim also belong to Landen Montgomery.*

Williams turned around and walked back over towards Montgomery and said, "Landen, you are going to have to cancel your plans and come with us to the station. We just received some more evidence, and we have a lot more questions for you."

Coming face to face with Williams, he said, "ARE YOU PLACING ME UNDER ARREST?!"

"No! But if you don't come now. I will take what we have to the district attorney...you don't want me to do that without getting your full story."

The truth was, Williams still had no evidence to even prove Ms. Mary had been murdered. All they had was proof that Montgomery had visited her. Any good district attorney would have laughed Williams out of their office if he presented them with what he had.

Montgomery huffed, "Don't use that line on me. I have used it a thousand times. I'm going to go into my house to call my attorney, and I'll meet you at the station in about an hour."

"Make sure you are there in an hour. If I have to come back, it will be with a warrant." Williams replied.

"Some friend!" Montgomery snarled, as he walked back into his house.

28

"Landen, you IDIOT!!" Craig Kingsley yelled. "I am not going to go down with you for any of this. How could you be so careless! I don't pay you to make mistakes. How are you going to fix it?"

"I have Detective Fields in my pocket. I'll offer him some more money to get rid of whatever physical evidence they have. No evidence, no case. As far as I know, there were no witnesses that saw me there."

Pacing the room, Craig said, "All I know, is you better fix it, and fast! I called my attorney, and he is going to meet you at the police station."

Montgomery threw his hands in the air and walked out of the room. He pulled out his phone and called Detective Fields.

"Fields, we need to talk!"

"I can't right now. I'm busy."

"If you are with Williams, I need you to make some excuse and get away for a few minutes. Do it NOW!"

Putting his hand over his phone, Fields said, "It's my wife. I need to take this. I will be back in a few."

"Take your time," replied Williams.

Fields quickly walked through the station and out the front door. He could barely make it to the sidewalk before he yelled, "WHY ARE YOU CALLING ME?"

"I need you to get rid of any evidence they have on me. I am authorized to pay you whatever is necessary for you to do so."

Looking around, Fields said, "Are you crazy! I will not tamper with evidence. You killed that poor woman, didn't you?"

"Don't get all self-righteous with me. You have broken the law more times than I can count over the past 6 months. If I go down, you go down with me, you got it? Now get the evidence and destroy it."

Fields pushed the red button on the phone, ending the call with no response. He walked towards the parking lot. He could not believe that he had gotten himself into this situation. There was no way he would do what Montgomery asked of him, but if he went to jail, he would lose his pension and his insurance...then what would happen to his son?

Fields walked down to the lab and started making conversation with the lab tech.

"I need to look at the evidence for the case we are working on," he said.

"If you came just five minutes earlier, I could have saved you from having to make a trip to the evidence department. I had my assistant take it down. You'll have to go sign it out if you need it."

Exhaling, Fields said, "Ok, I guess I'll have to make a trip down there. Thank you."

He turned and walked out the door heading towards the evidence room.

29

Sean started putting all the evidence neatly back into the box. He glanced at Karen's picture, and whispered, "I'm sorry, Karen." He sat her picture face down on the table and put the top back on the box. Sean cradled his face in his hands and walked in a circle. He walked back over to the box and took both fists and hit the top of it, putting a hole in it. He grabbed the lamp that was on the table and lobbed it towards the wall. White pieces shattered and flew across the room as it crashed. He leaned back on the bed, slid down to the floor and sat there with his knees pressed against his chest.

While he was down there, he began picking big pieces of the lamp off the floor. He went to throw it in the trash when the hotel phone rang. It was the front desk. One of the guests called about a loud, disturbing noise. Sean assured the clerk that everything was fine. He told them that he accidentally knocked the lamp into the wall, and they could add the damage to his credit card. The clerk offered to have someone come and clean it up, but Sean declined and said that he would take care of it.

After picking up the rest of the pieces of the lamp that he could see, he looked down at his watch. He had only an hour to be dressed and at the reunion. Sean swiftly put on his clothes and headed out the door. He went back and grabbed the box of evidence. He still did not trust leaving the box in the room. Sean walked to the front desk and said, "I changed my mind, I picked up most of the lamp, but if someone could go in and vacuum, I would truly appreciate it."

————

Landen Montgomery walked into the station. Behind him, was a thin man with unnatural black hair, an expensive smile, and an even more expensive suit. The officers started whispering as he was escorted across the station towards the interrogation room, where Detective Williams and Fields awaited their arrival. One police officer opened the door for them, and Fields and Williams stood up.

Landen's attorney slammed his black, leather briefcase on the table and said, "This is ridiculous and downright shameful, I can't believe that you have the audacity to drag this former decorated detective down to the same squad room that he interrogated hundreds of criminals and publicly embarrass him. I promise you I will have both of your badges when I am through!!"

Putting his hand up, Detective Williams replied, "Ok, ok, ok... please save the theatrics for the court room. We would not be here if your client hadn't lied to us."

Slamming his hand down on the table Montgomery yelled, "I did not lie! I told you I was at her home earlier that day."

"Shut up Landen, let me do the talking." Exhorted the attorney.

"Well, the evidence proves otherwise." Detective Williams replied. "We have a statement from Ms. Mary's nurse that she bathed Mary, changed her clothes, gave her pain meds and put her to bed."

"Ok, how is that proving that my client was lying about the time that he was there?"

"We have forensic evidence putting him at the scene after the nurse left." Detective Williams exclaimed.

"What evidence?!" Montgomery said, glaring at Detective Fields.

The attorney said, "Landen you say another word, and I'm going to walk out of here and you can find yourself another attorney...What evidence?"

Williams replied, "We found some hairs on Ms. Mary's night-gown that belong to former Detective Montgomery here. The nurse said that she changed Ms. Mary before she went to bed, so your client had to be there later that day."

Montgomery stood up, clenching his jaws and began to walk to the door. Then he turned around and yelled, "The nurse is liar, and I am not going to sit here and be insulted any further!"

"SIT DOWN NOW!!" yelled Fields. "You are a liar and you killed Ms. Mary!"

"Young man you better watch your mouth. Not only will I have your job, but we will sue you for defamation." Rebuked the attorney.

"I have proof," Lamented Fields.

Putting his head down, he said, "Williams, I need to talk to you and the sergeant."

Fields told Williams and the sergeant about the money he had taken to do favors for Landen Montgomery. He told them that he believed that the orders came down from Craig Kingsley, but he could not prove it. He never met or talked to Mr. Kingsley.

Softly, he said, "I needed the money. All of it went to Grayson's treatments. After I started doing little jobs, I was trapped. Anytime I told Montgomery that I was through, he would remind me of how much my family would suffer if anyone ever found out what I had done. I did enter Ms. Mary's house to get her to sign the papers. But let me make this perfectly clear, I would not take a life to save my son's."

The room was silent. The sergeant and Williams stared at Fields in disbelief, but they also wondered; if they were in Fields' shoes, what would they have done to save the life of their child.

Williams exclaimed, "Why didn't you come to me? I'm your partner. We would have figured out another way to get the money you
needed."

The sergeant cleared his throat. Behind his back, everybody
called him Sergeant Turkey because he had short arms, a very round
stomach, and very red second chin. He stood up out of his seat and
said, "Detective, you are in a lot of trouble. You just confessed to
some very serious crimes and made some very harsh statements
about a decorated detective, and my friend. Do you have any proof to
back this up?"

Fields replied, "Yes, I made sure that each time I took a job, I sent
confirmation to Montgomery, and each time, he would yell at me
and tell me not to do it again. I knew that one day I would need it. I
also have the text when I told him I would not take a life. That
conversation was the day that he asked me to Kill Ms. Mary."

The sergeant said, "Williams, I need you to get on the phone with
the district attorney...I want to make sure that before you go back
into the interrogation room, we have everything we need to make
sure this arrest sticks. I have no patience for dirty police officers or
dirty former officers. Fields, you leave your gun and shield on my
desk. I suggest you get in touch with the union as soon as you walk
out of my office. I am very disappointed in you. Your career is most
likely over, but hopefully you won't go to jail. I'm sorry about your
son, but nothing can excuse you abusing the power that the people
in our community entrusted you with."

30

Sean walked into the hotel lobby and was greeted by the reunion committee. They caught him up on all the planning and explained to him where he could go to make a donation towards the next reunion. He smiled and nodded, but there was no way he was donating anything for the next reunion. This is the first and only one that he would ever attend.

He followed the signs into the ballroom and opened the French door. Red and white balloons, streamers, and banners decorated the room. The biggest banner was placed above the stage; it was white with red writing that said: *Willow Run Flyers Class of 2003*. The room was filled with people laughing and bragging about their children, their jobs, and what they had been doing since the last reunion. Sean wished high school brought back happy memories for him, like it did for his former classmates.

Sean began to approach the stage, and there were picture boards on each side of it. He gasped when he saw a picture of him and Karen on prom night. He turned and made a quick exit to the door.

He made it out of the door, right when Lauryn, the president of the reunion committee, grabbed the microphone to speak. Sean's phone began ringing, and he pulled it out of his pocket, He answered, "Detective McKnight."

"Detective, its Williams. I told you I would call if there were any updates...for your information, I just slapped the cuffs on Landen Montgomery and took him down and booked him myself for the murder of Ms. Mary."

Sean took a seat in a plush, brown, black and gold chair in the lobby, "Are you serious? I knew that guy was no good."

"Sean, I know the reason you came was to solve Karen's murder. You must be frustrated that you weren't able to at this time, but if you had not found the hairs on Ms. Mary, Montgomery would have got away with murder. You should be proud of yourself, and I know that eventually, you will bring to justice whoever killed Karen. You are a fine man."

"Thank you, Detective Williams...and thank you for the box of evidence."

Sean walked over to the open bar. After seeing the picture of him and Karen, and then receiving the news about Montgomery, he needed a drink; he ordered a scotch. He heard a familiar voice coming from behind him.

"Hi, Sean."

He turned and replied, "Hi, Courtney."

Courtney stood there in her black, fitted dress, that had a split that went all the way up to her thigh. She sat up on the stool crossing her legs, showing off her six-inch Christian Louboutin's.

"I'm happy you are here, Sean, even if everyone else is not, I am."

"Thank you, Court."

Smiling, Courtney replied, "Court...you haven't called me that in a long time. I miss our friendship, Sean. Maybe one day we can be friends again."

"I doubt it, but it was really good seeing you."

Montel walked over to the bar, "Courtney, I have been looking all over for you! I told you to stay away from him, but you always seem to be up in his face. I know that the reason you were so jealous of

Karen when we were in school, was because you have always secretly loved Sean. Tell me how he would ever be able to give you what I can. He is a nobody; he was in high school, and he still is."

Sean stared at Montel and drank down the rest of his scotch. He wanted to punch him in the face, but he knew that is what Montel wanted. He sat his glass down, left a tip on the bar and went to look for table 29. At Sean's table, was Chanda Powers, a lady named Dawn with bright red hair, along with her husband, who had blond hair on the side and was balding in the middle. Dawn told Sean that they were in algebra together. Sean pretended to remember her so she would stop talking to him.

He wanted this night to be over so he could leave the very next morning. Chanda leaned over and said, "You have no idea who she is, do you?"

Sean shook his head sideways, and they both chuckled, earning a sharp stare from Dawn.

"What a beautiful brooch you have on, Chanda." Dawn said.

"Thank you, I only wear it on special occasions. It was my mom's. Can you believe this used to be a ring? Her fingers were much bigger than mine, so I took it to a jeweler to see what they could do, and he suggested placing it on a gold plate and making it into a brooch."

Sean glanced at the brooch and an eerie feeling came over him...

31
PHYLLIS POWERS PROM DAY
2003...

I'm going to find out what Chanda is hiding from me if I have to tear up every inch of her room. I have worked too hard for someone to ruin her future.

I tossed papers, clothes, anything that I could pick up from Chanda's once immaculate room. I could not find anything. Then I remembered that Chanda used to hide her diaries under her mattress. I lifted it up, and there was an envelope marked "Answers." On an index card inside the envelope was written: *Put answers on scrap paper before testing. My father has arranged for the proctor to get sick, and another proctor will go the day of our test. My dad does not know that I am sharing these answers with anyone, so keep your mouth shut, and you will be able to get into any college you want.*

I felt sick to my stomach. *What has she gotten herself into?* I slid to the ground, reading the card over and over again. I can't believe this...I did not raise Chanda to be a cheater. All that overtime I worked to get her tutors, and the money I spent on prep tests for her, and this is how she repays me.

Somebody must have found out. I jumped into my red Ford Escape and drove to Montel Kingsley's house. He had gotten my daughter into this mess. I want to talk to his father and find out what he is going to do to protect Chanda. His son's life wouldn't be ruined by this scandal, but my daughter's certainly would. I want so much for her; she would be the first one in our family to go to college. She wants to be an attorney. She told me when she starts working, I can stop.

I pulled into the long driveway and stepped out of the car. I ran to the door and pushed the doorbell three times. An older lady in a black uniform with a white apron opened the door. I insisted on talking to Mr. Kingsley; the lady kept insisting that he was unavailable. I pushed my way around her and went into the house.

Mr. Kingsley walked out of his office, "Excuse me! Who are you, and why are you in my house? I have a friend who's a police officer, and in fact, he is on his way over as we speak. I'm going to have him arrest you if you don't leave immediately."

I yelled to him, "I'm Chanda Powers' mom...I know about your son cheating on the test. We need to talk now!"

He turned around, nose flared, cheeks red. He waved me towards him, and we went into his office; he slammed the door closed. I went on to explain that Montel had given Chanda the answers as well.

He replied, "If you are here to blackmail me, you can forget it. My son will be okay, but what about your daughter?"

I stepped up so I was close to his face and said, "I'm not here to blackmail you! I am here to make sure you take care of this situation. Did your son tell you that someone found out about them cheating?"

"Yes, one of Montel's friends, Karen. I am going to take care of that tonight. Don't worry, no one will ever find out."

"They'd better not!" I said as I walked out of the office towards the front door. My heart was beating a mile a minute thinking about what he could have done to me in that room. He could have killed me, and no one would have ever known.

I got into my car and flew down the driveway. I swerved, and almost went off the side because some idiot decided to try to drive past me on this narrow road. I laid on my horn. It was a black car, that looked like an unmarked police car. It must have been the police officer that Kingsley was talking about.

There was no way that Chanda was going to stay at prom, not after this. All the sacrifices I made for her; I feel so betrayed. I pulled into the school parking lot and slammed on the brakes. I saw a girl running from the building. She is Chanda's height, but it wasn't her... this girl is wearing a beautiful, fitted green dress.

I got out of the car and met the girl. She started crying in my arms. I asked her if she was ok. I asked her name, and she said Karen. All I can see is red...

"You know my daughter, Chanda."

Karen pulled away from me. I grabbed her. She screamed, and I pulled my hand back and slapped her with the back of the hand that I wear my antique ring on. Karen began screaming louder. I opened my purse and grabbed out the knife that I carry for protection. After work I have to walk through an alley to get to my car at night.

Karen's eyes became big, tears poured out and black streaks from her eyeliner covered her face. Karen turned around and ran. I was not worried about catching up to her...I run five miles every day, and besides, Karen has on heels. The stupid girl should have taken them off. I hit her from the back and knocked her to the ground. She screamed, and I stabbed her. I stabbed her over and over and over again, until she was no longer moving.

I jumped up and looked around. There was a young man coming out of the auditorium, so I ran the opposite direction, and then worked my way back to my car. As I drove down the street to my house, I passed police cars driving fast towards the school, with their sirens blaring.

I pulled into my garage and entered in my kitchen. I walked to the kitchen sink and began to scrub Karen's blood off my hands. I put the knife in the dishwasher, and then grabbed a bucket, filled it with bleach and water and wiped down the inside of my car. I changed my clothes and sat on the couch with a bottle of wine, as I waited for Chanda to return home.

32

Sean jumped up, ran to his car and grabbed the photo of Karen with the mysterious mark and bruise on her face. He could not believe it; it was the exact pattern that is on Chanda's brooch. He pulled out the witness statements again and read what the hall monitor, Paul Stewart, told the police. He said he thought he saw a red car pulling out of the parking lot. He remembered because the tires screeched, causing him to look behind him.

Sean dropped his head...he remembered that Chanda picked him and Jordan up for school before in her mom's red Escape.

In a fog, he slowly walked back into the ballroom over to the table and sat down. Chanda said, "Sean, are you ok?"

He looked up and whispered, "No, Chanda, we need to talk."

———

Chanda began hitting Sean and yelled, "You are a liar! There is no way my mom could have done this."

Sean pulled out the picture of Karen with the bruise on her face, and Chanda started to rub the brooch. She was vigorously shaking her head side to side and said, "It's all my fault. She must have found out."

Sean said, "What are you talking about? She found what out?"

"In high school, Montel and I cheated on our ACTs. Montel's dad paid off one of the proctors. We swore we would never say anything, and then Montel foolishly told Karen, and she was going to expose us. Montel went to Karen and tried to talk some sense into her, but she would not listen.

Montel said that we had to make Karen look like a liar, so he paid Jordan to get Karen alone...and he started kissing and hugging her. I took a picture and then walked over and started yelling at them both. I told Karen I saw it all; that she was flirting with Jordan. I was on the committee for prom, and I was in charge of the slide show, so I was going to add the picture in it. We figured that if Karen did talk about Montel and I cheating, it would have appeared like she was just saying it to get revenge.

Then Montel told me to tell Courtney what I saw, and that I took a picture. I had no idea she would react like she did. At prom, Jordan told Montel that he was going to tell you what happened, and that's when they got into the fight. After Karen was murdered, all three of us decided not to ever tell anyone what we had done. I'm sorry, Sean."

Montel, Courtney, and Jordan came out and began walking towards Sean and Chanda.

Montel said, "Chanda, are you ok? What have you done now, Sean?"

Sean had Karen's picture clutched tightly in his hand. He shoved it as hard as he could into Montel's chest and yelled, "Look at it! You may not have been the one who stabbed Karen, but you are definitely complacent in her death. I know everything. I know you are a cheater and a liar. After I go to Detective Williams with this evidence, I will be contacting the local news to give them a story about how a college cheating scandal led to the death of Karen LaSalle."

Sean turned around and walked away. He took his phone out of his pocket and called Shelia, "Honey, I did it. I am on my way home."

ABOUT THE AUTHOR

Dee McQueen was born in 1975 in Ypsilanti, Michigan. She published her first Fiction book on March 6, 2023 entitled -Detective McKnight- Deadly Engagement. Deanna began writing at a young age. She wrote short stories, poetry, and plays but her passion is writing mysteries. Deanna worked as a paralegal for several years. She is the mother of 3 beautiful children and 1 grandson. She also has a business, By Deezign Mysteries, where she writes and host murder mystery parties.

Made in the USA
Monee, IL
13 April 2024

56571880R00080